Caged in Darkness

J.D. Stroube

Copyright © 2011 J.D. Stroube

All rights reserved.

ISBN:1466362367
ISBN-13:9781466362369

LCCN:

DEDICATION

I dedicate this book to my Father, who taught me that no matter
how many times life beats me down; I can rely on him to pick
me up. To my Husband, who is unfailingly patient with my
peculiarities, and who pushes me to succeed at every step I take.
I love you both. I would also like to dedicate this book to my
cats, who spent endless hours curled up with me on my rocking
chair, as I wrote this. Their company is a safety blanket for my
soul and my family is the rock that keeps me grounded.

CONTENTS

ACKNOWLEDGMENTS

This book would not have been possible without my amazing support network. Thanks to my family for supporting me, to my talented cover artist Regina, and my friend Lisa who helped me through the editing process!

1 PROLOGUE

Sludge caked my bare feet and slowed my passage. Nature hindered my flight, as though wanting me to turn back; to go to *him*. It had turned hostile. The stillness that calmed me during sleepless nights, the breeze that cooled my angry flesh, and the moon that guarded against nightmares were now my enemies.

My sanctuary no longer comforted me. It was a predator and I its prey. My heartbeat broke its ordinary rhythm and cried in its claustrophobic state. My lungs smothered the worn organ, utterly failing to provide oxygen as I flew through the forest. I refused to stop even though my veins melted away to acidic fire. I needed freedom.

My dress strap caught on a branch and was torn free. I felt a twinge of pain as the edge pressed into my shoulder and drew blood. Chaotic laughter trailed behind me. It turned the ageless trees into a bitter menace. They loomed around me to conceal *him*. Branches tore again at my skin in an effort to bind me, while weeds sought to shackle my ankles. The pain they caused was minor when compared to the searing inferno at my core. I clawed through the barriers, crying out when I came to a dead end.

Towering rocks blocked my passage and *he* was gaining ground. I made an attempt to pull myself over the stone barricade, but they sliced through my palms. I desperately tried to find leverage, but I was winded and my strength had left me.

My mind was betraying me; my natural instincts at war with my purpose. My body and soul screamed for survival. Though it wasn't mine I was fighting for...

2 SAVANNAH'S JOURNAL

First entry: Recounting my past

I would love to say my life in Meadow Falls was blissfully ordinary, but that would be a lie. I yearned to wake in the morning excited for the day to begin, instead of waiting for it to end. It is said that you can't miss what you've never had, but I think that is what people say to make themselves feel less guilty about their own happiness. Personally, I conform to the saying "the grass is always greener on the other side." The grass on my side is stale and brown with patches of dirt that have never seen the sun.

There are people in the world, who are just *wrong*, and then there are the masses that are *right*, or at the very least they lie in between. I do not belong to any group. I don't exist. It's not that I have no substance; I have a body like everyone else. I can feel the fire when it burns against my skin, the rain when it caresses my face and the breeze as it fingers my hair. I am just empty, *inside*.

How does someone's psychological makeup create the person they become? Why did I have to be barren of emotion? Why did my parents conceive a child when they never should have? I have yet to find a book that can explain to me, why I picked the short straw. How does fate decide who will be given a life of privilege, against the child who must scavenge through the garbage to find their weekly dinner? Why couldn't I have won the celestial lottery and been given an entirely different life?

The world is not fair. If it were, I would have been given a choice on the life I would lead. Life is supposedly filled with paths that enable unlimited choices. That is a blatant lie. No one has freewill until they are an adult, and by then the choices that were made for them have already set them on a passage that limits the choices they have yet to make. Adults are merely given the illusion of free will. The course of their lives has a set destination, which was dictated by their previous experiences and the foundation their parents built for them. Although, some might say that is just my excuse to ignore the person I have become.

I have rules that govern my life, which have kept me from being the type of person that harms others. They are numerous and often overwhelming, but there is one rule that supersedes all others, which is to never become a *monster*. The day I look in the mirror and see a monster, is the day I give up my struggle to survive.

I prefer to keep to the fringes and watch while others attempt to make connections. The fewer I have, the easier life is. I have perfected the art of matching the emotions of others, but always wearing a mask is tedious. Some relations were chosen for me; my guardian, Maye and her foster son, Ash. There is only one link I chose, and her name is Willow.

I saw Willow be beaten down by society and forced into the same shadows that I inflicted on myself. I loved the shadows; the feel of them slithering over my body and curling around my limbs was comforting. Willow hated them. She longed for the light, but was only allowed to touch the fringes.

I was ten years old, when I made the decision to become her friend. At first, I was afraid that she would ask questions about *before*, but she never did. Eight years later she has never asked and I have never offered. She seemed to naturally understand that I needed a portion of my life to remain separate from my past.

I think of my childhood in two separate stages: the time before I was safe and the time after. I didn't always live with Maye. I was born with a mother and father. It wasn't until I was a bit older that I understood my parents were different from other parents. Other children did not need to raise their hand to ask permission to talk. They were not locked in a cage to keep from complicating their parents' lives. They were given typical punishments, such as being grounded or having a time out. Other children did not have parents who practiced the dark arts.

My parents were raised in a community of witches. The coven did not practice the dark arts, and instead used their gifts to the benefit of others. My parents were inordinately powerful witches, but were not satisfied with the power they had been gifted. The more they used their gift, the more addictive the magic became. They were similar to drug addicts. They built up a tolerance to their particular drug, and now required more power to sate their cravings. My parents were drawn to the dark arts to sate their addictions. They didn't seem to mind that black magic comes with a price.

When the community discovered my parents' use of the dark arts, they were repulsed and banished them. They firmly removed my parents from influencing the other members of the coven, but didn't realize my mother was pregnant with a daughter.

Those who practice black magic are not always evil. Usually, dark witches fall into shades of gray. However, my parents were firmly grounded at the darkest end of the spectrum. Twice a week, until I was nine years old, I witnessed my parents sacrifice the lives of innocents. Their screams would echo through the house and reverberate against my eardrums until my mind would fracture. With each fracture I lost a piece of my soul until I became lost and empty inside.

When my parents were without an innocent to sacrifice, they spent their time finding other ways to entertain themselves, which usually included focusing their powers on me. Living energy would emerge from their flesh and envelope them in a haze of darkness. When they focused the mist on me, the evil would gather around until it found a fissure to wither through. It would invade my body and corrupt any piece it could find that was still pure. When the darkness dispensed itself from my pores, it would take that bit of innocence with it. My soul screamed at the loss as it was torn from me.

When I was nine, my parents made a mistake. They allowed me out of my cage. Nine years of being subjected to their never ending abuse had turned me into a feral being. Luckily, my intelligence was not hindered by my feral nature. My parents were distracted when they released me from my cage to bathe. The smell emanating from their neglect had become obnoxious.

I learned years before that fighting them was senseless. They thought me meek and obedient. *I wasn't.* When my mother shoved me into the bathroom, I landed on my side and allowed a breath of pain to escape. I knew that was what she was waiting for. She enjoyed my pain; monsters usually do. The bathroom on the main floor had a small delicate window in the shower stall. It was bubbled glass, which ordinarily provided privacy, but now provided my escape. My parents were about to perform one of their rituals, and I knew from experience that this one was loud. The house was enspelled to contain sounds, but that didn't stop the noise from spreading to every corner within it.

This was my chance. I turned the water to full and I examined the metal towel bar. Over the years I loosened it, in expectation that I might use it to escape. Grabbing hold of the toilet plunger to use as leverage, I managed to pull the bar loose. It didn't take long to burst through the glass, and use a towel to brush away the stray pieces that remained.

The opening was petite, but so was my frame. Nine years of neglect and malnourishment had ensured I would be tiny. I grasped the edges of the frame and pulled myself through. It was difficult. I made it through the window by pure determination.

My feet hit the ground and I tore across the grass. I was surrounded by homes, streets and signs. I didn't understand this world. It was loud, due to a lifetime of sensory deprivation. The sound of cars flying through intersections and children screaming as they played in the street disoriented me. I covered my ears in a halfhearted attempt to block out the unknown. My mind was swallowed by the rush of senses I was experiencing.

I knew the name of the village my parents grew up in, and had seen a picture of their old coven. My escape plan was limited. How would I find freedom in an unfamiliar world? Who would help me? I was quickly realizing that my escape was short sighted

I knew I needed to make a decision. My parents were distracted by their ritual, but I didn't know how long that would last. I looked in all directions, and noticed a woman loading her trunk with some luggage. There was barely enough room left for me to fit, if I squeezed into a tight ball. I waited until the woman went back into her house, ran over to the open trunk, and squeezed my small frame into the back beneath a blanket.

I tried not to panic at the length of time I was entombed within the trunk. I could hear each car that passed, faint country music from the radio, and occasional noises I didn't recognize. The trunk was filled with a pungent odor: a cross between stale bread and mildew. Eventually, the car came to a stop. I held my breath as the trunk opened. The woman let out a squeal when she saw me, and then a sigh when she realized I wasn't a threat. It took her a few minutes to take in my appearance, before she raised her hand to her mouth.

A building beside a large highway lay behind the woman. Benches danced around the building beneath the sparse trees, and cement walkways led to a set of doors. A sign next to the walkway, directly behind the woman, said "Rest Stop".

"I need to get to a place called Meadow Falls." I rarely had opportunity to speak, and wasn't sure how to greet a stranger, let alone a woman who unknowingly aided my escape.

"Little one, what happened to you? Where are your parents? Why are you in my car? Did someone hurt you?" She looked around at the only other people near the rest stop, and lowered her voice. "Do you know your home phone number or address?"

The woman had kind eyes, but she was overwhelming me. Her questions were stringing together and I couldn't process them. My hands lifted to cover my eyes from the blinding sun.

My parents rarely allowed bright lights within our home, and the sun was like needles in my corneas. I swung my feet over to sit on the edge of the trunk and considered what to say.

"I needed to escape them. My parents are..." I paused, swallowed, and began again. "I need to get to my other family. I didn't know what else to do." I paused, while I waited for her to say she was going to call my parents, but she had a knowing look in her eyes.

She sighed. "What's your name?"

I wasn't sure if I should give her my real name, but decided she couldn't do much with a first name. "Savannah."

I knew what she saw when she looked at me. I was nothing like my name. Savannah sounds exotic, beautiful and special. I was a nine year old child, who looked closer to seven years old. I had long ratted hair that hung in clumps down to my hips. It was impossible for her to tell the color of my hair with the grime that coated it. I wasn't even sure I knew what color it was. I knew that the woman saw a child, who looked closer to a skeleton with a layer of skin. My eyes were bruised, lips cracked, and my cheeks were sunken. The only redeemable trait, that made me look more than a pile of rags, was my liquid silver eyes ringed with violet.

In that moment, with this kind woman framed by the sun's rays, I felt that my life could someday be different. That it was possible for a malnourished waif to turn into someone completely ordinary.

3 ESCAPE

Third Entry: Safety

When Maye issued the council meeting, the adults from the surrounding houses gathered in the casting circle. Outsiders from nearby districts drove to Meadow falls and joined the coven to discuss my situation. The adults clustered together in the circle surrounding the altar. The outsiders revealed themselves as representatives of the sister covens. It was decided that my parents were a poison that needed to be eliminated, and the covens would band together to be the antidote.

That night Maye made certain my parents could never hurt another. She took me in and promised to never allow anyone to harm me. The expression on her face was heart wrenching. Her clothes were scorched, and she had a gash across her right cheek. She moved slowly, not due to physical exhaustion, but rather emotional drain. Her hunchback seemed to be tied to gravity; she was bent over as though a ghostly weight lay on her shoulders.

Maye closed the distance between us and encircled my shoulders to hug me. To others it would look as though she were comforting me, but she was the one who needed comfort. I would have preferred not to be touched, but I forced myself not to stiffen at the contact. This was the woman who had saved me. How could I deny her one moment of human comfort?

Part of me wanted to ask what had been done. Were my parents dead? Was it a quick death? Would they ever be able to hurt me again? It was difficult to imagine a life free of their constant abuse. I suffered the eternal fear that even if they were dead, they would find ways to inflict pain on me and those near me. Was it possible to wage war from the afterlife? I craved answers to these questions, but I couldn't bear to ask Maye. I knew she was hurting and my questions would bring her more pain.

Maye became my surrogate mother, as she had already been for Ash. His parents died in a car crash when he was four. Maye, as his Aunt and closest relative, became his legal guardian. She was the only family he remembered. I wish it was that way for me. What I would give to slip into blissful ignorance. Unfortunately, my parents were a nightmare that was repeatedly inflicted on me in daylight and in sleep.

When I first came to live with Maye, I felt guilty that she and Ash needed to suffer my presence in their lives. They had a simple routine that they followed, and I barred their usual routine with my presence. Theirs was a beautiful home that I infected. They no longer had peaceful nights. The echoes of my childhood screamed through the hollowed essence of their home. They often came down to breakfast with false cheerfulness that was ruined by the ashen circles beneath their eyes. My nightmares plagued my dreams, and their wakefulness.

My bedroom was upstairs with a large bay window, and a bathroom that connected mine and Ash's room. Maye originally gave me the guest room on the ground floor, but without any windows and only a single escape route, I panicked. Maye understood the unusual situation and switched rooms with me, for which I was grateful.

I quickly learned to lock both doors when using the facilities to avoid uncomfortable interruptions. My first week in my new bedroom, I casually walked into the bathroom as Ash was drying off from the shower. Rather than have that happen again, we both opted to be cautious. I knew the bathroom acted as a tunnel for the sounds that came from my room at night. My nightmares, which were in fact memories… must have affected him. To hear that pain, and only have a bathroom as a barrier between him and my taint must have been exhausting.

I became a ghost, misting through their home, while avoiding as much interaction as possible. Occasionally, they would notice an item that had been moved, or leftovers that were eaten, but those were the only clues to my presence. I often envisioned a medium coming to their home to banish my existence, or a priest to exorcise my demons. I wanted to keep my interruptions to a minimum.

It wasn't until my sixth month there that they became fed up with my avoidance issues. I slithered into the kitchen for some food. It was around midnight, and my new family was waiting for me. The kitchen was abnormally large with oak cabinets and a long counter that divided the kitchen from a dining room. This was not to be confused with the larger dining room, whose doors were always closed.

Maye was sitting at a table in the room beside the kitchen. It was a circular structure with one leg shorter than the others. The table wobbled whenever something touched the top of it, but was stable enough to eat at.

Ash leaned against the counter, while popping grapes into his mouth and looking amused at my obvious confusion. I couldn't understand why they were waiting in the kitchen. It was late, and I knew from experience that this time of night was the safest to leave my room.

I paused next to the counter on the opposite side from Ash. It helped to have a barrier between us. "Why are you both up so late? Do you want me to come back later?"

Maye snorted, and swiveled in her chair to face me. "Dear, this is an intervention. Do you know what that is?" Her voice was a bit hoarse with a tint of annoyance.

I knew what an intervention was. My parents had limited my education, but since coming to live with Maye I had been sucking up as much knowledge, as my mind could handle. I spent every day closeted within my room reading any book I could get my hands on, which made me grateful that my mother had originally employed a nanny who taught me the basics.

"Yes, I know what an intervention is…" My voice trailed off and I looked at Ash for a clue to what was going on and he shrugged. "I just don't understand why you think I need one."

Maye lifted her frame from the chair and crossed to the counter. She stopped at the end and acted as a physical bond between Ash and myself.

"Child, you are part of this family now. You cannot keep hiding in your room; it's unhealthy. This has gone on long enough and it needs to stop. Are you unhappy here? Have we done something to make you feel unwelcome?" Her hand reached across the counter and folded itself across my own; I yanked mine away.

"No! Oh, God no. You're the best. You and Ash are the kindest people I have ever known. If it wasn't for you, I'd still be living in a physical portrait of hell. I love being here. Please believe that!" I felt guilty that they didn't know how grateful I was. I made a mental note to make a greater effort to include myself. I had no idea how to do be part of a family.

Ash shifted his feet and looked at Maye, and he nodded. "Savannah, we don't want you to leave. We want you to start hanging with us. I mean, we are a family. Normal families eat together, they watch TV, and… I don't know… they get sick of each other and argue. You only come out at night, and whenever you see us you agree with everything we say. It's kind of weird." He wrinkled his nose, and continued. " It's not that we want you to start doing something you are uncomfortable with, but ummm… maybe stop acting like a crazy person who is afraid of people. We don't bite. I promise." He snickered. "At least I don't. I can't make any promises about Maye." He cocked an amused grin at Maye, and grabbed another grape.

Maye sighed, while shaking her head. "I do not bite. I just nibble a bit." She then glared directly into my eyes. "Child, we want you to be happy. I already suggested you have counseling with a member from our sister coven that specializes in psychiatry, but you refused. If you can't find natural paths to help heal, I am going to insist on her treating you. What happened to you before is horrifying, but you have a chance here to live a normal life. You can have friends, find a hobby, go to school and even learn magic."

At my blank expression, she continued. "What you are or where you came from is not important. It is who you are and the choices you make, that determine who you will become. If you can look inward and be satisfied, the opinions of others should melt away."

I knew I would never be someone who is comfortable enough with other people to develop friendships, and I wasn't sure that anything interested me enough to become a hobby. However, the last two options made me pause. I had never been to school. School was for normal kids, with normal lives and normal problems. I wanted that. Magic on the other hand was at the opposite end of the spectrum from normal, but in this town... abnormal was the new normal.

I looked across the counter at Ash and then at the end of the counter to see Maye. They both fixated an expecting look on me. I wanted those things; I just didn't believe that I was capable of them. I had spent the past nine years bound in a prison of eternal darkness. My parents had torn through my innocence and left me with a tar-like substance that was corrupting what was left of me. I could feel it at night; slithering and curling around my soul as it slowly devoured me.

4 GOTHIC

Fourth Entry: My Ghost

The day I first came to Meadow Falls is little more than a dream, though that little girl plagues me every day. I still hear her crying out, and my skull fractures as pain is inflicted on her. She remained frozen in an eternal chamber of torture, and I did not know how to help her escape. Though, *I* would never escape *her.* She would follow me around for the rest of my life; a ghost waiting in the wings for me to acknowledge her. Her soft trailing fingers would continue to attempt a connection that I refused to allow; that I couldn't allow if I wanted to survive. That ghostly girl was weak and insecure, while I needed to be strong and confident.

Current Day
15 years, 11 months, and 14 days old

When I slammed my locker door shut, my friend Isabella was leaning against the lockers with an irritated expression on her face. Isabella, or as she preferred to be called, "Izzy," was a recent edition to mine and Willow's antisocial group. Izzy transferred to Meadow High her freshman year, and immediately took to us. It wasn't that surprising since Izzy was peculiar. She used to live in New York City, which was more accepting of eccentric personalities. At first, we barely tolerated her. Willow and I were completely happy with our duo and didn't need to make it into a trio. However, after Izzy invited herself to our homes and conveniently showed up when we were out, we decided to accept the inevitable.

Izzy had a beauty that could not be replicated. She rarely wore anything other than black and was always decked out with bizarre jewelry. Today she was wearing a short black dress with bright red straps and a flared skirt. Her blonde hair was cropped short in back and angled forward to end at her chin. She never wore make up, which suited her translucent skin and bright blue eyes.

Despite her slightly gothic appearance, her personality was more cheerful than people would expect. She wasn't the most agreeable person and had no patience for the bleach blonde Barbies of our school, but she had a sense of humor. She was also extremely loyal and accepting of mine and Willow's differences. She never asked about the "witchy" part of our lives, but we knew she was aware of it. She had been to our homes and seen our town in the woods with the altar at its center. She seemed to naturally understand that it was a topic that was off limits.

"Where's Willow?" I snapped to attention at my best friend's name and shrugged.

"She sent me a text letting me know she was going to be late. She said she'd be here in time for lunch."

Willow was a mouse with a secret spunk. She was eternally shy, but was the sweetest person I had ever met. I would do anything to keep her happy and safe. Her parents were part of the Meadow Falls coven, which meant she had lived there her entire life. Until I came along, she had been completely alone. The other kids in the coven tolerated, but ignored her. She wasn't particularly talented in the magic arena. However, all born witches only had a portion of their true power until they came of age.

On the 16th anniversary of our first breath, we would come into our true powers. Until then it was impossible for the witchlings, which is what we called the children of full grown witches, to know how powerful they would be. Though, power tends to run in families. Willow came from a weaker line, and therefore was invisible to other witchlings.

Willow's family was less powerful, but had a rare gift that allowed them to bring people back from the brink of death. That gift only came in handy if they were present for the exact moment of death; when a person passes through the veil between life and death.

I looked up when the warning bell sounded. Izzy was staring past my shoulder with a hungry look in her eyes. I turned around to see a dark brooding senior leaning against his locker speaking to someone, who I assumed was Griffin.

The senior was casually dressed with a maroon, long sleeve button up shirt that hung open to his middle. The shirt revealed a tight v-neck that accented his muscles. His hair was short and slightly spiky with a messy attitude. His eyes were devouring; I knew from experience that when those eyes were fixated on you, you could feel yourself being pulled into their vortex. His eyes were mesmerizing and kind. Most girls wanted to fall into those green orbs, but I was not one of them. Ash may be the most beautiful guy I had ever met, but he was the closest thing to a brother I had.

Izzy had issues with being interested in guys who were off limits to her. Ash, being part of my family, was off limits. He was also a senior, which made him even more tempting since seniors rarely dated sophomores.

Ash always acknowledged Izzy, which just encouraged her infatuation. She didn't seem to understand that he was kind to her mainly because she was my friend. My anti-social behavior never sat well with Ash. He would go out of his way to bring any sort of happiness to my life. He appreciated anyone else who did this and so he was grateful to both Willow and Izzy. Though, Willow didn't seem to enjoy his attention quite as much as Izzy did.

I eyed the boys as Griffin slammed his locker door and turned his sandy brown haired head in our direction. His blue eyes turned cold, when he took in Izzy and me. Ash looked up to see as he walked to us. Griffin stopped a little past us and waited impatiently as Ash leaned towards me to brush a wavy strand of hair away from my face. I shook my head so that the strand would return to its original state.

Ash smiled and said, "Maye wanted me to tell you that she wouldn't be home after school. She said she had some things to take care of."

Ash and I had a tentative relationship that was built on his unfailing patience in the face of the wall I built between me and the outside world. Ash's problem was that he never gave up and he had a soft spot for damaged goods. I was the poster child for damaged, which meant that in our own way we had developed a close bond. He constantly tried to bring me out into the light and I persisted on remaining one with the shadows. However, there were times when we compromised by meeting in the middle.

"I know. I overheard her on the phone last week; something about a lawyer... Did she say why she was seeing one?"

Ash grunted, "No, but I wouldn't worry. She's probably making a will or something." He stared me in the eye for a moment. "Do you want me to go straight home after school so you're not alone?"

Ash knew that when I was alone in the house I tended to have panic attacks. He learned that the hard way when he came home with Maye from seeing a movie, to find me curled in fetal position in the kitchen pantry. When they tried to comfort me, I slashed at them with my nails, while letting forth a growl. My mind simply wouldn't process who they were, and as cornered animals do... I viewed them as a threat. Ash managed to lure me out of my internal rage by singing to me. When my mind began to process who I had been slashing at, I broke down into tears. They made a point not to leave me home alone again.

"Mmmm... nope." I avoided his eyes, as I shoved my books into the tote at my feet. "I'm not going to be home anyway. I promised Izzy we could go dress shopping today." I rolled my eyes at Izzy.

"Well, if I am going to be seen with you two wallflowers, you can't look like you just rolled out of bed. It's either wear my clothes or buy something new. Since you and Willow insist my wardrobe is too garish for your complexions; that leaves shopping…" Izzy shrugged with a smile and walked off towards her first period class.

Ash blocked my way when I tried to follow. "You're going shopping?" He laughed, "To a mall… to buy real clothes?" Amusement and disbelief ran rampant in his voice.

I shoved Ash gently against the locker. "Yes, to the mall for *real* clothes. What kind of clothes did you think I was going to buy?" I crossed my arms and gave him my, *be careful what you say or you'll regret it* stare.

Griffin came to Ash's rescue by shouting that they needed to get to class or they would be late. Ash glanced at me, shrugged and said "Guess I can't answer that question. Talk to you tonight, S."

I looked in the direction that Izzy had gone and slowly ambled forward. This was going to be a long day. Not only did I have to worry about a calculus test and the inevitable bruising from self defense class, but I had to worry about shopping too.

Ash

When Savannah turned, her hair grazed my face and brought the fresh scent of strawberries. I thought it was ironic that she was firm in her decision to be anti-feminine, considering that she added small accents, which were very much feminine. Savannah had been that way since the first day I met her. She fought a war within herself; always trying to be someone she wasn't. She was beautiful, but she hid it behind baggy clothes. She was smart, but she never opened her mouth to show it. She was insecure and yet she deliberately took the lead, as if daring her personality to deny her anything.

At first, I was jealous when Savannah came to live with us. I had been uncomfortable with the idea of sharing Maye since she was the only family I had left. When I thought of the look in Savannah's eyes the night she showed up on our lawn; the vacant cavern of emotion behind her gaze, I wanted to rescue her.

I was a child when Savannah came to live with us and didn't realize that she couldn't be fixed. She wasn't a disease or a broken computer; she was a girl who had endured the nine circles of hell and survived. I admired her, but more than that I loved her. I had to share Maye, but I gained so much more.

I couldn't help but feel protective of Savannah; it was in my nature. I was an Emmons; it was in our blood to protect our loved ones, just as it was in our nature to descend into a poisonous rage when those loved ones are threatened. The thought of the trials Savannah endured, was enough to make me lengthen my fangs and hiss.

I walked to English, and went to each of my classes, but they were more of a formality at this point. Other than first period English and fourth period gym, I had enough credits to graduate. Rather than taking a course load of unneeded electives, I choose to go home directly after lunch.

As a senior, I sat in the first cafeteria. My small band of friends took up the table in the middle of the room, which meant that we were the object of many stares. Unlike my friends, I was uncomfortable with people watching me. I felt like a stage puppet for the student population. Griffin enjoyed performing for everyone. I didn't.

My table was filled mostly with girls and a handful of guys. I sat on the far end of it, which over looked the entrance to the cafeteria. Griffin sat directly across from me and Isis next to him. The rest weren't witches, and remained unaware of what we were.

Isis was a member of the coven, but I found her annoyingly flirtatious. Her cruelty towards Savannah and her friends made me dislike her. Many considered Isis beautiful, but her beauty lay in her appearance only. Her skin was the shade of bronzed coffee. Her hair hung straight down her back to graze her thighs, and her eyes were like red garnets. She wore her makeup the way ancient Egyptians had, with the color outlining her eyes to make them seem catlike. She had an amazing body; thin with long legs and big breasts. I knew that was why Griffin kept her around. They hooked up on a regular basis, but neither really wanted the other for anything more than sex.

Isis was rarely found without her two best friends, Jen and Stacey. They were twins from the coven, but their parents had taken them out of the country to visit relatives in Ireland for a few weeks. Isis was alone and she did not look happy about it. She was on a war path and her personality depicted it.

I winced, thinking that Isis would probably go out of her way to cause problems for Savannah until her friends were back to distract her. She usually attacked Savannah when she was in a bad mood.

"Look who just walked in." Isis craned her neck, as she pointed out Savannah entering the cafeteria. "It's such a shame that she has the body of a child. She could almost be pretty. Maybe I should suggest a plastic surgeon to fix her problem areas." Her eyes sparkled with wicked intent. "I mean, she is almost sixteen. It's not normal to be so flat chested. Maybe, she is really a boy?" Isis looked me in the eye, daring me to defend Savannah. I ignored her, and ate my fries.

"I think I'll offer her that advice." Isis turned to Griffin. He nodded, and smiled.

"Go ahead. It's about time someone told her." He nodded in Savannah's direction.

Isis pulled herself out of her seat and began to walk towards Savannah with a gleeful determination to her step. I spun out of my seat, walked briskly to her and grabbed her arm in a harsh grip.

"Lay off it. You're not going to say anything to her, understood?" I ground the words through clenched teeth, and felt my eyes glow in warning. I was descended from the Emmons line, which was known for their tempers.

To be on the bad side of an Emmons was deadly. I was strongest in the fire element, and when push into a rage my teeth would lengthen to poisonous fangs. We were known to be especially protective of our families.

Isis stared in wonder at the fangs protruding from my open mouth. Her mouth was wide at seeing them for the first time. Ordinarily, I controlled my temper, but lately I found my emotions chaotic.

"You will leave her alone." My speech was slurred. Isis nodded, and I released her arm. Her arm was bruised in the shape of my fingers. I should have felt guilty, but seeing Savannah walk out the doors and I knew I couldn't regret my actions.

Savannah

The first half of the school day passed quickly. I hardly noticed as the hands of the clock danced past noon. The lunch bell sounded and my stomach growled in annoyance. I stored my bag in my locker on my way to the cafeteria and took a few moments to check my cell for messages. I had a text from Maye and felt my stomach drop before I opened it.

Considering Maye's bafflement at modern technology, I knew she must have spent a good while figuring how to send me a text, which was confirmed when I saw several more texts with the exact same message. It took seeing my parents' names flash across the screen before I processed what she wrote me. Nausea engulfed me, as I stuff my phone into my locker and rushed to lunch.

Our basement level school cafeteria was somewhat unique. It was divided into four sections, which were then divided into cliques.

The first section was filled with the stereotypical jocks and Cheerleader's, but also had people who I called the *shadows*. These were people who were notorious for shadowing these groups and were tolerated, but not encouraged by the actual group members.

The second section was filled to the brim with the *norms*, which were people who were literally the definition of average. Usually they refused to stick to a single clique, dangling between several.

The third cafeteria was littered with the smart crowd. These were not just typical geeks, but rather truly intelligent individuals. The last cafeteria was the unlucky one. Anyone in that section belonged in the invisible or obnoxious category. They were either so mouse like that no one noticed them or they belonged to the worse category filled with class clowns, Goths, or Punks. While the great population shunned the people in the last section, I found them to be the most worthy of knowing.

I walked through sections all four sections and paused when I reached the doors that led to the quad. My best friends were unquestionably *section four* students, but rather than be persecuted by high school stereotypes; they choose to ignore their status. We compromised with high school mentality by claiming a picnic bench outside during the warmer months and populated the library during winter.

Our bench was a mint green metallic monstrosity, but it was ours. During lunch, we were usually surrounded by herds of people who claimed the benches nearby. However, today I noticed that most of the benches were empty. I figured this had something to do with the light mist that covered the benches from the spring rain this morning.

Willow and Izzy were seated on opposite sides of the bench. This was usually the case since I was the thread that tied them together. Izzy was the obnoxious borderline Goth type, while Willow was the invisible moral type. They belonged at opposite sides of the spectrum, but when the three of us were together they glided from their opposing sides to merge in the middle.

Willow seemed distracted this morning, while Izzy chatted uncontrollably. When I approached, a branch snapped beneath my flats and caused them to turn. Willow looked up at me and smiled. Most people couldn't see Willows beauty because she caved in on herself when around other people. However, when

Willow wasn't afraid that people might be judging her, she had a natural classic beauty.

Willow held her smile a bit too long and I noticed the strain behind her hazel eyes. Her chestnut brown hair was casually thrown into a messy bun at her nape with random strands falling around her heart shaped face.

Willow never wore her hair up unless it was arranged perfectly. She wasn't the typical teen to concentrate on what was fashionable, but instead kept to a durable look. I knew something must be off about today; her hair was screaming it at me. I made a silent promise to ask her later. Willow knew my silent signals and quirked up the corner of her mouth. Willow had coupled her messy look with a pair of loose fitting jeans and a shirt that was at least a size too big on her.

"Hey, S." Willow's voice was quiet and soft. She was the embodiment of nature; quite, serene, and its beauty was often overlooked. If there had been any noise other than a light breeze on the nearby trees, I would not have heard her.

I sat down next to Willow and directly across from Izzy. Willow grabbed a lunch tray and pushed it towards me. I glanced down at some Bosco sticks with marinara sauce and garlic fries. Since Willow had a free period directly before lunch, she could get to the lunch room before the absurdly long line took over. Luckily, she knew exactly what to order for me on any given day. She claimed we had a psychic appetite connection. I thought it was more likely that it had to do with my picky appetite, the fact that I only liked five things on the menu, and I hated eating the same thing two days in a row.

"Excited about shopping?" I said this sarcastically Willow disliked shopping even more than I did.

Willow rolled her eyes and rasped "Oh, of course. I've been anxiously waiting for this day! Or rather the end of it..." Izzy grabbed a rolled up napkin and threw it at Willows face, and Willow batted it away.

"Ha ha, very funny you two! Just wait, when we arrive at the bonfire and everyone stops to stare at our gorgeously clothed bodies, you *will* thank me." Willow and I exchanged a horrified glance and burst out laughing. Izzy may want everyone staring at her, but if they did that, it would only be in revulsion. People attending the bonfire were not overly fond of our little group.

"So, where are you planning on taking us for our little field trip? The strip in Landing or the mall in Bloomingdale?" I already knew the answer, but I also knew Izzy would have a riot talking about our excursion, which would provide me with time to think about more important subjects, while I nodded absently in affirmation.

Maye wasn't giving me a choice. Her text said "We are going to your parents' house this weekend", not "I would like to" or "Are you interested in." She had made her text a statement and when Maye did that, the subject was not to be argued. I wouldn't be given any leeway about confronting that place. For whatever reason, Maye required me to face my childhood for the possibility that I *might* want some of their things. I thought that was ridiculous, but I couldn't tell Maye that.

My heart constricted, as I remembered Maye's text. As their only child, my parents' estate had been left to me when they died. Maye, as my guardian, had been in control of that estate all these years, and we had silently agreed that it was a subject I did not want to talk about. However, according to her text, she had a buyer who was interested in my parents' home. She knew that I would like to wash my hands of that house and accepted the offer on my behalf. She wanted me to go with her to the house this weekend to see if there was anything I wanted to keep before papers were signed.

I wondered what the house would look like now. As far as I knew, it hadn't been touched since the night my parents' lives were extinguished. Would my cage be there? Would it stand erect, surrounded by tacky wallpaper and grime coated windows. Or had Maye have removed it already?

I wasn't sure I could face the memories that home carried. They would echo through the barren existence of that house. I knew from experience a home like that bled a soul of all happiness. I wasn't certain I could retain that place again without succumbing to the imprinted memories my parents had left me with. Would the taint spread? Could I infect others with their remembered evil?

"And I thought we could buy some tissue paper, cover it in mud, and use it as belts to whip all the boys into shape with."

"Huh? What about tissue paper and whipping?" Willow snickered softly, while Izzy stared me down with her parental, "don't mess with me" face. She was testing to see if I was listening and I failed.

Liam

My coven was congregated in an overly large barn that my mother designated for our rituals. Ordinarily, my afternoons were spent being home schooled in both the traditional and witch ways. However, today as the High Priestess of the Sacred Moon coven, my mother called a meeting.

It was rare for us to convene for reasons other than rituals. Since, we didn't have a ritual scheduled for today, they were puzzled and worried. We hadn't set up for the amount of witches attending this gathering. I sat to the side on a barrel of hay, which was the only type of seating available. I had no desire to mingle with the others.

As the son of the High Priestess, I was frequently plagued by women in the coven, who wanted to exploit my connection to my mother. I wasn't interested in a serious relationship and if I showed interest in a member of the coven I would be expected to commit. I chose to only see non-witches because those relationships came with no strings attached. Luckily, the human population was overrun with sexually frustrated women, who considered me the bad boy type. I never wanted for company, and I did not need the complications of the type of company I would find here tonight.

My mother, Diamante climbed the stairs to the stage at the back. She commanded their obedience without saying or doing anything. They simply quieted at the sight of her.

"I'm glad to see you're all here. We need to address an issue and it cannot wait since there is limited time to court her. The child of Irena and Devon Cross, is about to ascend." Diamante paused for the coven to react, and proceeded. "I know you must be surprised, because I have kept their child a secret all these years. However, I did not wish another coven to learn about her existence and stake a claim on her. Unfortunately, it has come to my attention that another has."

The assembly of people began murmuring, a sign that my mother's capabilities were being doubted. As the High Priestess, she was expected to uphold our coven's best interest. A witch with Cross blood in her veins could have brought an obscene level of power to our collective.

Bored, I began inching away from the wall to leave the room. I wasn't interested in politics or my mother's plotting. I was almost entirely through the exit, when I heard my mother say my name.

"Liam has agreed to help us fix this issue."

Hearing shouts that questioned how I could possibly help; I couldn't help wondering the same thing. I thought back to the past few days and… nope. I did not suffer an injury that would cause memory loss or poor judgment, and that was the only way I could be expected to help my mother with anything. I wondered how she expected to ensure my cooperation.

"The Cross girl is an adolescent, which means she is likely to be guided by her hormones and nothing more. Girls at that age don't care about anything other than themselves and boys. This is how we can be certain she will choose us for her initiation. Liam will seduce her into falling in love with him, and when she does, she won't dare choose another coven for fear of losing him."

Oh, God. My blood began to rush, while a roaring began in my ears. I saw black, as I ground my teeth and induced a migraine. My *mother* expected me to pimp myself out to a teenage witch, who had mostly likely been a pampered little princess from the day she was born. The Cross family was one of the highest lineages in the paranormal community. Famous, Rich, and Royalty; meant that she would probably be a spoiled, opinionated ditz, with no idea what the real world was like. I couldn't believe my mother expected me to seduce *that*.

After the coven dissipated, my mother found me in her suite. The floor was evidence of my continued pacing, while waiting for her to finish with the coven.

"What the hell do you think you're doing?" I asked. "Offering my help to the coven, without even speaking to me about it?"

"What's the matter? At least we will finally put your womanizing talent to good use." Diamante challenged. She sat at her vanity and pulled her black hair down to brush, while looking at me in the mirror.

"I only date non-witches. There is no way I am helping you with this scheme. You want me to seduce a 16 year old? Are you crazy?" I crossed my arms and leaned against the post of her four poster bed.

Diamante pursed her lips. "I have understood your rebellion. I haven't asked for you to take responsibility, as my son. I've let you do what you want, when you have wanted, but this is enough. You will do this for me. It's for the best of the coven, which means it is for your own good." She spun in her seat to face me.

I studied her face, taking special note of the anger in her eyes. She didn't permit members of the coven to question or refuse her. I was the only one who dared, and as her only son she allowed me some leniency.

"It won't work. I seduce, but I don't romance. I wouldn't know the first thing about making a girl fall in love with me. You should get someone else to do it."

"I trust *you* to do it." She stood, and walked over to grasp my hands. "You're my son. The others would view it as an insult, were I to ask anyone other than you. Besides your seduction methods tend to convince women that they are in love with you, rather than recognizing their feelings as lust. We just need her to believe she is in love with you, long enough for her to take her vows." She took my chin in a painful grip and forced me to look at her. "You will do this, or never ask for anything from me again."

I couldn't look away. I knew when I was dealing with my mother and when I was dealing with my High Priestess. Right now, she was not my mother and I could not refuse my Priestess.

"Of course I will do ask you ask." I bowed my head in defeat, and she smiled. She was my mother again.

"Make sure you ask the cook to make you something to eat before you leave. Too much junk food isn't good for you." She turned her cheek for me to kiss.

I walked away feeling that my will had been stolen.

Savannah

Later that afternoon, Izzy surprised me by taking us to the strip in Landing, rather than the mall. She must have been taking pity on us, because normally she would jump at the chance to subject us to a day of endless shopping at the mall.

Izzy parents had gifted her with a beat up rust colored Pontiac for her 16th birthday. The air conditioning didn't work, but the stereo did and Izzy thought that made the car a dream. It didn't matter that the Pontiac had seen more birthdays than she or that it was a gas guzzler, as long as she could listen to music she was happy. On the other hand, Willow and I were miserable. By the time we pulled up to the strip, we were anxious to begin shopping if it meant relief from the heavy metal beating away at our ears.

Izzy led us towards a store called "The Gothic Tea Party", which I considered an oxymoron, but made sense once entering the store. I gazed around at the strange assortment of clothing. The store was filled with clothes that merged designer with classic gothic and punk. I've heard Izzy wax on about this store ever since it opened six months ago, but I didn't really believe anything she had said.

I was surprised to find that the mirage of apparel appealed to my inner fashionista or at least the tiny part of me that wanted to wear beautiful dresses. It was strange that it took gothic meeting couture to make shopping fun. Next to me, Willow gazed around her in surprise. She met my eyes and we both looked to see Izzy beaming at us.

Izzy was in her element as she buzzed around the store, collecting dresses in an array of colors featuring mostly black, burgundy, and silver. Occasionally, she would walk up to Willow or me to hold a dress against us to see if it was flattering. During these examinations, she would purse her lips and nod as though having a conversation with her mental fashion twin.

Willow and I walked around absently, occasionally trailing our fingers against an outfit here and there. The night before Maye had given me enough money to purchase a small wardrobe, knowing that I rarely wanted to go shopping. Maye took advantage of the occasion and made me promise to buy more than just a single dress. I guess that meant I was turning Goth couture. I wondered what Maye would think of my odd choice in clothing.

Willow paused suddenly and effectively brought me to a stop when I nearly tripped over her.

"She's never going to let us live this down, you know." Willow whispered, nodding in Izzy's direction. "Maybe we should at least pretend that this is torture."

I snickered. "She'll never buy it. Besides if we do that, we can never come back or she would suspect." I shrugged. "Did your dad give you enough money to afford this place?"

I knew that Willow's parents didn't have a lot of money; a fact that she was embarrassed about with anyone other than me.

"I think so. I'll just make sure I pick something that I can afford. If I have to, I'll wear something I already own." When I started to offer to cover the difference, Willow covered my mouth with her hand. "No. I do not accept charity. Do not even think of offering what I know you were about to offer. It's too tempting and would just make me feel guilty later."

"Fine, suit yourself, but if you end up with an outfit you hate because it was the only thing you could afford, don't take it out on me." I stuck my tongue out at her before signaling a sales lady.

A slightly irritable sales woman escorted us to changing rooms. Izzy perched against the room across from mine and delivered the expected exclamations of pleasure at seeing each of us in a wide range of gothic clothing.

While in the dressing room, I examined myself in the assorted outfits. Usually, I avoided mirrors. When I first came to live with Maye and saw my skeleton frame, I decided it was pointless to assess my image. When I bought my clothes, it was usually at Goodwill, thrift stores or garage sales. Those places did not come equipped with a dressing room.

I wore a long black skirt that hung to my ankles and had a slit on my right leg that reached the highest point of my thigh. The waist of the skirt ended in a V shape beneath my naval. The top matched the skirts style perfectly. Its sleeves hung off my shoulder like drapes that layered down my bicep. My midriff was barred to an inch beneath my breasts.

I knew I had matured over the years but was surprised to see a perfect hourglass figure with a strong flat belly. My black hair hung in natural waves around my face and fell to the middle of my back. The light brought out my natural blue highlights. My eyes were captivating. The violet surrounding the iris was the same, but the silver was more prominent. I was surprised to see that my features complimented one another.

My beauty had been passed to me from my mother. I was almost sixteen and never compared my physique to hers, but I could see the similarities. Ordinarily, I would contain my mass amount of hair in a butterfly claw or ponytail. It was rare for my hair to be loose, and even rarer for me to wear clothing that showed my body to its advantage. I wanted to be attractive, but I wasn't sure it was worth the cost if the coven began to associate me with my parents.

Would Maye love me less if she saw my mother looking back at her? Would Ash think less of me if I began dressing like every other teenage girl? Would Willow be disappointed that I had succumbed to the teenage stereotype my worth is judged by my beauty? Would I think differently of myself?

I promised Izzy I would buy a dress to wear to the bonfire and I promised Maye that I would buy a flattering wardrobe. One of my many rules is to always keep a promise, which means that regardless of the answers to my questions; I would buy the clothes and would ignore the consequences until they presented themselves. I gazed in the mirror a final time, and realized that I would never be comfortable showing my midriff.

When the three of us left the store we carried more bags than I would have thought possible. Willow fell in love with an outfit that was slightly out of her price range. She allowed me to pay for the difference as an early birthday present, since I usually spent more on her anyhow. She reasoned that this way I was actually spending less money on her. I bought more clothes than I owned in my entire life, and Izzy bought the right to tease us incessantly for the rest of our lives. Not surprisingly, Izzy was the happiest.

Izzy paced ahead to unlock the car, while Willow and I were weighted down with bags that hindered our pace. My neck began to tingle, and a cold draft of air trailed down the curve of my spine. Hair flew into my face with an invisible force and I began to sway dizzily. I had the intense feeling that I was being watched. Not just that someone was staring at me; it was as though someone were invading my body. I shook the feeling away and sped towards the car.

"S, are you okay?"

I came to the front passenger side door and lowered my hair so that it covered my face. There was no one watching that I could see.

"Savannah?" Willow pushed against my shoulder, and I shook my hair behind my shoulders to face her. Her brows were furrowed in concern.

"I'm fine. I just thought I saw someone I recognized." I attempted a fake smile and slipped into the car.

5 HIDDEN FOR A REASON

Fifth Entry: Day Terrors

Shopping had been more enjoyable than expected, but I wasn't fooling myself that I would enjoy tomorrow. Part of me resented Maye for putting me in a position that I would need to go back to my parents' house. However, she had given me so much that I knew I would find the courage.

Savannah

Izzy dropped me home after a quick dinner and I immediately took to my room. I could hear sounds coming from Ash's room, but his door was shut. Not wanting to disturb him, I choose to closet myself in my bedroom.

My bedroom was fairly bland for a teenage girl. I didn't see the point to decorating a room that was literally just a cube I slept in. The headboard of my twin size bed rested against the far wall. A nightstand stood to the left side of the bed with a small lamp and alarm clock on top. A dresser hid behind an overly large bookcase overflowing with books. To the right of my bed was a small walk in closet that was mostly empty. On the opposite side of the room was a large bay window that opened up onto a miniature terrace. Not surprisingly, the terrace was my favorite spot and housed some patio furniture and a tiny space heater for brisk nights

Maye and Ash thought that my room represented my need to remain apart from the family and they altered it slightly to make it seem more lived in. The picture frames of my friends and family were placed on my dresser by Ash and the flowery quilt with matching drapes had been Maye's addition. I came home one day from a hike through the woods to find the *surprises* in my room. Each time I saw their personal touches; I couldn't help but think that they were symbols of love and the only items I cherished.

My bedspread was twisted, as I moved to the Carrie Underwood song on my MP3 player. I was lying on my belly, attempting to write a biography on Marie Antoinette. It would be more interesting if it was a biography about Carrie, but I had a feeling my history teacher wouldn't be too happy with that.

I looked up to find Maye peeking through the doorway with a smile on her face; her wrinkles in stark contrast to her emerald eyes. They were not to be outdone by the crease between her eyebrows, which announced the impending serious conversation.

"How was your day, darling?" She moved forward to sit on the edge of my bed, while I put my pen down.

"Which part do you want to hear about first, the part when I am fairly sure I flunked my calculus test, or when Izzy brought us to a gothic clothing store to torture us, and we ended up loving it?"

Maye let loose a startling laugh, "Please tell me, you are not going to begin coating your eyes in black coal and walking around looking like a corpse." When I didn't say anything she raised her eyes in a disbelieving stare.

"Well, I did buy clothes, but they're not exactly the typical gothic look. I think you would approve and they actually suit me." I shrugged, as I pushed my homework aside. "Is that really why you came up here?"

Maye chuckled, "You're too smart for me; you always were." She sighed. "I am assuming you saw the text I sent you earlier today?" I was silent, but nodded in ascent. "Good. I found a buyer for your parents' home, but I think that we need to make a visit to the house before we sell it."

"Why? It's not like I want anything that belonged to them!" My anger began bubbling up and Maye looked around in surprise to see my furniture shaking in response. "That house is supposed to be, what...a legacy from them? It's a legacy I want nothing to do with." I ground my teeth, and sat up to look at Maye. I tried to calm my anger and saw the furniture's shaking dwindle to miniature spasms.

"Child, I am not bringing you there for your parents' legacy. I am bringing you there for your ancestral legacy. You shouldn't turn your back on your ancestors just because your parents took a dark path." Maye fixated me with a stern look, and shook her head in disappointment. "You of all people should know not to judge someone by who they are related to. Your line is filled with extraordinary witches who have passed down heirlooms that belong to you."

"Couldn't you just go and bring me back whatever you think I should have?" Silence greeted my question, and I hesitantly began to explain, "I'm not sure I can face that place again. I don't know what it will do to me. Please don't ask me to do this." My head bowed in personal shame at admitting my weakness.

"Darling, I will be with you. Your parents are gone; they can't hurt you. All that is left to bring you pain are the memories. If you face those, you'll be free. You can't spend the rest of your life hiding from yourself; always afraid that your memories will incapacitate you, and they will if you continue to bury them." She gripped my hand, while her eyes flowed with a river of emotion.

"Why do I need to face the memories in that house? They already plague me every night in my dreams? I can't escape them."

Maye looked disappointed, "Sweetheart, you know I love you, and part of loving someone means that sometimes you need to save them from their self. You are not confronting the memories in your dreams. The nightmares are your minds attempt at repressing demons that refuse to leave."

"Okay, okay. You win, but before I agree to go, you have to promise me one thing. If I want to leave, we leave. I'll face my demons, but on my terms."

"Agreed." She smiled and kissed my forehead. "If you were strong enough to become the woman you are, after being subjected to such evil, you can overcome any obstacle." She walked slowly from the room and closed the door behind her.

Her faith in me was eternal. I never knew unconditional love and support until I came here. Maye and Ash had given me more than a home; they took my fractured soul and somehow pieced it back together. The damage was still done, but now I knew I could survive. I wouldn't fail them.

My body became overwhelmingly lethargic. It was as though the stress that had built up over the course of a lifetime was suddenly slamming down on my shoulders, and forcing me to kneel before the memories. My eyes drifted shut and I passed into a dark sleep filled with nightmares. My mind swam with blurry images of my parents committing horrendous acts, and switched to visions of red eyes following me as I ran for safety. I continuously turned and each time I was confronted with a new image that left me whimpering beneath the sheets. I was becoming fitful, when something cool grazed my cheek. A soothing sound quieted me into a restful sleep and I was at peace.

I woke to the sound of my alarm clock indicating that it was 8 o'clock. It felt much earlier. The sun shone through the glass, which made my room look larger than it actually was. I opened the bay windows to step onto the terrace. The rush of damp morning air refreshed me, but I couldn't tarry long. I could see a storm coming in and did not want to be caught on the terrace in a downpour.

The terrace connected to Ash's room, and I looked over to see his window open. He must have been out earlier. We met here most mornings. We rarely spoke, but instead sat in warm silence. It was my favorite part of the day. He never pressured me to talk and understood that I needed those moments.

I followed my weekend morning routine; showered, brushed my teeth, threw my hair into a messy bun, and replaced my robe with a pair of jeans and a billowy t-shirt. Before leaving my room, I opened the dirty clothes hamper and pulled my money and student ID from the jeans I wore the day before.

I walked into the kitchen to be confronted by the obnoxious odor of burnt cinnamon rolls, cooling on the stove top. Ash bent over them and poked each with a fork, as if testing to see if it would move.

I cleared my throat and he angled his head away from the rolls to greet me with a slight smile.

"I think I killed them." He nodded towards the charred remains of his attempt at breakfast.

"I think that's a safe assumption. I vote don't risk it."

Ash folded the rolls into a paper towel and threw it into the trash with a thud. I sat on the counter and grabbed the glass of milk abandoned there.

Ash arched his right eyebrow, "Feeling lazy this morning? I guess that means, I am setting out everything for breakfast?" He sighed, and flashed a sarcastic smile. "Since you're drinking my glass of milk, I suppose I have to make do with a can of orange juice, since that was our last clean glass?"

"Mmmm... good milk." I smacked my lips. "You could always do the dishes and have a glass of milk too." He walked over to where I sat, and placed his hands on either side of my waist.

"Or I could take back what is rightfully mine and you could do the dishes." He made a grab for the milk and I artfully pulled my hand holding the glass as far away from him as I could.

"Fine. You get the darn milk." His arms were back in their original position and he stared directly into my eyes, while I brought the milk back to my lips to take another sip.

Guilt rushed over me. I smiled and hesitantly offered the glass to his lips. He took a sip. His mouth quirked into a half smile.

"You're too easy. Keep the milk; I poured it for you anyways."

Laughing, I swatted at his back with the kitchen towel that lay on the counter. He began combing the cabinets for assorted boxes of cereal, bowls and sugar. I watched as he placed them on the table in the connecting family dining room, and added fruit, nuts, and bread to the mix.

"Hope you're okay with dry cereal?" He didn't glance up to see my nod.

Pushing myself off the counter, and moving around it I ran directly into Ash on his way back into the kitchen. Our feet tangled and before I knew it, I was plunging towards the antique tile. Ash grasped my waist with one hand and my hip with the other. He held me in a position that mimicked the type of dip couples generally did at the end of a dance.

"Klutz." He kissed the tip of my nose, and pulled me back to stand before him, but I was dizzy from the movement and fell against him.

Ash's eyes widened, as my body molded to his. I quickly sucked in my breath. My face angled upwards and his lowered. Our noses grazed one another's in an Eskimo kiss. We stood still, his breath gently brushing my lips, and I noticed that he had specks of brown in his green eyes.

He straightened suddenly, and pulled my body away from his. My confusion greeted his detached stance, and noticing he moved closer. His hand, which had been holding my upper arm, slid upwards to pull the part of my t-shirt that covered my shoulder, to the side. He then leaned forward and placed a small kiss on the exposed skin between my shoulder and neck.

His breath grazed my earlobe, "As I said, klutz." He laughed awkwardly and went back to sit at the table.

I didn't know what was wrong with my body, but I felt warm. My spine was tingling from when he had kissed my nape, and my chest felt weighted down.

I vaguely wondered what Ash had meant to get from the kitchen, as I moved to sit across from him at the wobbly table. Before I could ask, Maye entered in her normal bubbly mood.

"Morning!" She stopped at the counter and poured her morning cup of coffee, took a testing sip, while gazing at us over the rim of the mug. "Did I interrupt something?" Her eyebrow arched in a way that always reminded me of Ash.

Ash quickly responded, "Nope." He shoved the last bite of Frosted Flakes into his mouth and moved to bring his empty bowl to the kitchen sink.

I grabbed an apple, from the bowl of fresh fruit Ash placed on the table earlier and watched as he leaned back against the sink behind Maye.

"What were you two chatting about then? The room feels positively frigid." She feigned a shiver.

"I believe we were talking about how I am a klutz and Ash is bull headed, or something like that." I jumped up from the table and walked to the dining room side of the counter. I looked at Ash innocently, expecting him to comment, but he didn't. Instead, he looked away and began to leave.

I frowned at his back, but he stopped in the veil between the kitchen and the hallway leading to the front of the house. He looked over his shoulder and said, "I promised Griffin I'd meet up with him and I'm already late. See ya later." Ash then looked me directly in the eyes and disappeared into the hallway.

"Bye!" Maye and I shouted in sync.

"What was that about?" I asked Maye, though I don't know why I thought she would have the answer.

"You tell me. I wasn't the one in here talking to him. Did you sleep well?"

"At first, no. Later I did though." I polished off my apple and addressed the elephant in the room. "What time are we leaving?"

Maye paused between sips. "We are going to leave as soon as I finish my cup of coffee. Be a dear and fetch my shoes. The black flats with the little swirls on the side."

I headed to the room in search of her flats. While sorting through the debris of shoes tossed haphazardly into a pile at the back of Maye's closest, I came across an album.

On the cover of the album was the name "Cross", which was my line. I opened the album to the first page to find a family tree, which dated back to the original members. When I continued to turn, the family tree was replaced by drawings, then portraits, and eventually pictures of people. I grabbed the album and the shoes.

After placing the album beneath the covers of my bed, I jogged downstairs to greet Maye. She was waiting at the door with her car keys in her hand and a large tote over her shoulder.

"Good, you found them!" She beamed and sat to place the shoes on her feet.

Our ride to my parents' estate was riddled with silence. Too many emotions overwhelmed me and Maye seemed tense. It wasn't long before we pulled up in front of the house. I sat still in the seat after the car went silent and built the courage to go inside.

Ash

I climbed into my SUV, but didn't put the car in drive. I looked out the windshield at my house. When Savannah fell against me it had been difficult to pull away. Our noses touched and I felt a pounding need to close the space between our lips. I wanted to taste her.

I shook my head; trying to wipe the thoughts from my mind. When she first came to live with us, I was protective of her, but over the years we had become closer. She began to eclipse everything in my world, which is why I needed to stop these kinds of thoughts.

Last night, I woke to Savannah's nightly screaming, but it was worse than usual. In response, I tried to quiet her. She had been in a deep, fitful sleep and remained unaware of my presence when I slipped into her room.

Careful not to wake her, I eased myself onto the bed and her restless movements quieted. I held her face, smoothed her cheek with my thumb, and sang lightly in her ear. Savannah curled her body around mine.

I felt strange being in her bed when she wasn't aware I was there, and tried to detach myself, but she pulled me in closer. I laid on my back with her legs tangled in mine, and her head resting on my chest. Her smooth legs twitched, and I gently eased her shoulder away, but she lifted her head.

"Ash." Her eyes were mere slits. I paused in the hope that she would fall back to sleep. "Ash…"

"It's me."

"Mmmm… stay." Her voice was barely audible, as she grazed her lips against mine and her head fell back against the pillow into a deep sleep.

I don't think she remembered her actions from last night, but considering my reaction to the memory, my body did. I spent most of the night calming her with my presence and voice. However, at dawn I managed to remove myself and get back to my room. It had been a painful night. I winced at the memory.

My best friend, Griffin was usually the one who had the heightened sex drive. Lately, mine had kicked into high gear when I was around Savannah. It was beginning to worry me. Maybe Griffin was right and I needed to get laid, but I was never one of those guys who had casual hook ups.

Groaning, I pulled out of the driveway. If there was ever a good time to visit Isis, it was now. Somehow, the relief that she would provide, left a bitter taste in my mouth. Instead, I turned my car towards the preserve. Maybe a walk would clear my head.

Savannah

I mimicked Maye's foot placement towards the deceptively plain house. The lower section of the house was multicolored stone and the upper portion was painted light yellow. A wraparound porch gave the home a Victorian air. The grounds were unkempt from neglect over the years, but the house was still beautiful. It stood calm against the suburban storm raging around it. The thunder screamed across the sky slapping the clouds into a heated turmoil that flew towards the south.

I wasn't surprised my parents' estate took this long to sell. From the outside it looked like an ideal family home. However, its history was not conducive towards "baby making" and family holiday dinners.

My mother and father had been discovered on the property; their lifeless forms frozen solid against the kitchen tile. Horrified expressions were taped across their features, and strange markings left angry welts against their flesh. Maye kept this information from me until she felt I was strong enough.

The police came to the house to investigate my parents' deaths and found the answer to serial vanishings in the area. In the basement, the police found a giant freezer filled with vials of blood from each of my parents' victims. The police found evidence they considered proof of their involvement in a cult. The world pronounced my parents, as participants in a serial killing spree, encouraged by a satanic cult. They were considered the greatest mass murders the state had ever seen. That was one point I completely agreed with. This house was not a home to build happy memories, but a museum echoing the nightmares of my past.

Maye pulled a key from the chain around her neck and opened the front door. I stepped forward, prepared to enter when the faint smell of sandalwood incense wafted through the opening to tease my memories.

The door opened into a dark foyer with a small den to the right and a large dining room to the left. I thought that once I was inside, the panic would consume me, but instead I felt detached. I couldn't hear the younger version of me screaming in horror or my parents' victims begging for mercy. The house was barren, and I was vacant of emotion. My parents had taken everything from me. They hadn't even left me enough to react to the destruction of my innocence.

The den was where my cage had been kept; it was gone now. Most of the furniture had been sold, but a few items remained. The books were still housed in wall sized bookcases, my parents' altar was still in the dining room, and a rocking chair leaned in the far corner of their library. These were the only pieces of evidence that someone had lived here.

"I'm going to look around in the basement. I am sure you would rather not go in there." Maye cupped my cheek with her palm and looked me in the eyes. "If it gets to be too much for you shout out for me. I'll understand."

I nodded. "I think I'll be okay. Um, what kind of items should I be looking for?" I bit my lip and gazed around in puzzlement.

"Just follow your instincts. Your blood will lead you to what is rightly yours. Don't worry about the books. I'm going to have them transferred to the Meadow Falls library in the morning."

I watched Maye's retreating back, as she opened a door and descended towards the basement. The idea of her being in that torture chamber gave me the chills. Maye was the essence of everything my parents had not been. The idea of someone I love entering a place filled with such hate, did not sit well with me.

She wanted me to follow my instincts, but there weren't any to be had. I considered what to do first. I could go room to room, floor to floor, or just randomly pick rooms until I had seen them all. One thing was for sure, the kitchen would be my last stop. I wouldn't be able to look at the tile without imagining my parents' blood flowing between the cracks. Though their deaths did not haunt me; I had enough death to last a lifetime.

Turning right, I entered the den. It was a bland room with wooden floors. I could make out the scratch marks my nails had left on the finish, and shivered. From what I remembered of this room, there wasn't anything special about it. Now, without any furniture to give it a lived in air, it was even drearier. Trailing my fingers across the dusty drapes, I followed the length of the walls all the way around until I approached the library door. Maye had said not to worry about the books, but in truth the library was the only room I had fond memories of.

Before my parents became the embodiment of evil, my mother occasionally had a maternal side. The memories were faint, but I remembered her reading to me beside the fireplace. As I aged, my mother's mental state deteriorated and her chaotic mood swings came more often. Eventually, her sanity was completely immersed in evil, and there was no sign of the mother who taught me to read.

The rocking chair we used to curl up on was in the corner now. The fireplace was dead, and the floor contained scorch marks. I sat down on the burgundy rocking chair. My horrible memories crashed down around me. The tears came quickly and drifted down my cheeks to land on the velvet chair. Not wanting to stain the velvet, I leaned forward to bury my face in my hands and let forth a keening cry. It was the cry of a wounded animal, a woman who just buried her child, and a little one who lost their first pet. It was a cry from my wounded soul.

My breath came in pants, as I tried to stifle my tears. Brushing the salty moisture from my flesh, I looked down at the rug beneath the chair. When I leaned forward, my only thought was to save the chairs fabric, but I hadn't noticed the rug enough to protect it. The strange thing was that I didn't remember seeing the rug, until after my tears fell onto it. A memory teased my mind and I vaguely recalled learning about the royal lines among witches.

There were ten royal families who were the first witches. The Cross family was one of the most powerful of the royals. Maye had told me during one of my lessons that the royal lines had learned to protect their secrets by ensuring that only one of theirs could find them. They used blood, sweat, saliva, and…tears to do this.

I pulled the chair toward the middle of the room and knelt beside the rug. From a distance the rug looked Persian, but up close it was more like pixels that didn't quite blend together. It was like looking at a photograph so closely that it no longer resembles a picture, just fragments of random colors.

I half expected my fingers to pass straight through the rug, but they felt solid wood when I touched it. There was a board on top of the real floor that was half an inch high, and camouflaged by the rug. Why would my parents go through this much trouble to hide something and yet make it so obvious that it was there?

The board wasn't difficult to pry away, and once it was removed from the space, it looked like an ordinary board. In its place was a tiny indentation in the floor. It revealed a small lever resembling an elongated door knob. I didn't hesitate; I reached to pull the lever, and the bookcase against the wall, glided forward and to the left. It left a hole that was barely big enough for an adult to fit through.

I vaguely wondered if finding this lever had been the type of instinctual feelings Maye had talked of. The secret pathway was jet-black. It was difficult to imagine light ever being held within its walls.

Thanks to modern technology, I was able to use my cell phone as a flashlight. After I tugged the phone from the pocket of my jeans the pathway lit up. It revealed a narrow hallway. Cobwebs and I imagined spiders, hovered around as I moved forward.

Pointing my cell phone towards the back wall, I kept my right hand on the wall to make sure I didn't miss a turn and to brush the webs from my face. I could still feel the silk graze my neck and shoulders. After about 300 feet, I felt a draft graze my bare arms. The source of the draft was a small rectangular room. It resembled an attic in an ancient house, with cobwebs connecting various artifacts that were layered in dust and the occasional sheet draped furniture.

A five foot long metal chest sat in the middle of the room, and when I tried to open it I found that it needed a key. A bar similar to a ballet barre connected two walls, and was filled with garments and bizarre robes. Some of the clothing looked like it was from the Renaissance period.

From a bookcase, I pulled out a leather bound text with torn pages that were literally falling apart at the seams. Sifting through it, I discovered it was journal from an ancestor of mine. In fact, all of the books looked like journals from various ancestors.

In a vanity, I discovered antique jewelry with strange symbols inscribed on them. I touched a necklace with a ruby stone at its center. It felt as though someone had warmed it with their breath. The other jewelry was similar. Some burned at my touch, others were icy, and one of the rings made me lightheaded. I found a choker necklace with a pentacle dangling from it. The pentacle was inset with small blue sapphires. When I placed the choker around my neck, my body became infused with warmth.

A bracelet with the Triquetra dangling from it caught my eye, and was soon attached to my wrist.

A table layered with strange items was placed next to the vanity. There was a bowl, ink, stamps with designs I had never seen before, a small stick shaped object, and a bone with a needle attached to it. I made a mental note to ask Maye about the items later.

I looked around, and even though my cell lit up some of the room, darkness had begun to ingest the light. Shadows danced across the walls and vines slithered up my legs. I could smell my parents' taint here and yet I was drawn to this place.

In the corner nearest to the entryway, was a box that resembled a casket the size of a china doll. Unlike a casket, it was made entirely of clear quartz with a large bloodstone imbedded on the lid.

The light shown on the casket and I watched as gray smoke shifted within. When I drew the light away, the shifting became more furious, but calmed when I brought my cell phone next to it. I noticed inscriptions carved into the quartz and the bloodstone. They looked similar to Egyptian hieroglyphs, but I was almost certain they were something entirely different.

I began to trace the inscriptions, but felt I felt a feathery touch against my other hand. I thought little of it, but shook my hand. The feeling persisted. I looked down to find a coffee colored spider with extremely long legs crawling across the back of my hand. I screamed and shook my hand furiously. In my attempt to get away I slipped, landing hard on the quartz box; the lid slid off.

Smoke swelled from the container and encased the surrounding area; effectively shielding half of the room. It lightened to a mist and ascended to the ceiling, where it spread to sheath the plaster. It made the room look like an upside down haunted house. I turned to run from the room, but hands grasped my shoulders in a viselike grip.

A shriek tore through my vocal cords when the hands pulled me back against a solid chest. The fog evaporated and I noticed the darkness surrounding me. This darkness had texture and twitched frequently. A harsh breath blew against my ear. The hands tightened and I began to worry they might crush my bones.

"Let me go!" The hands fell away from my flesh, but the body didn't move.

"All you needed to do was ask." The voice was deep with a slight edge and it sent tingles up my spine.

Before I could lose my courage, I spun around. I stood in shock at *what* I saw; and I don't say *what* lightly. Backing away from the *thing* in front of me; my back hit the wall. I was trapped.

The room was crammed with its sheer size. Before me was the body of a man with enormous wings, and strange eyes. In the dark they glowed with amber light.

Without wings he still would have overpowered the room. Abnormally tall with a strong torso, he was intimidating. His wings folded outward in a crescent shape that surrounded me. He was clothed in a pair of black dress pants, but his chest and feet were bare.

He moved like a bird; twitching and bunching his shoulders. His head angled back and forth to watch me, and as he did, his biceps tightened. His dark hair was chin length and concealed most of his face. His mouth was wide in a disturbing smile that displayed his perfectly white teeth; the upper and lower canines sharpened to fine points.

"Please, don't hurt me." I squeezed my eyes shut, hoping that when I opened them, he would be gone. My hands clenched into fists and I opened my eyes.

It was chuckling. While closing the distance between us, his wings spread out to blanket the wall behind me. He sniffed the air around my face and paused to stare into my eyes.

"I smell you." He growled.

His growl deepened and he barred his teeth in an angry snarl. "I *smell* your power." I watched, while his pupils dilated until they pushed away all traces of color. His hand reached for my neck, but when it came into contact my skin he let out a sound of anguish as his palm smoldered.

His face changed then. One moment he was divinely beautiful and seconds later I watched as his veins blackened to a cryptic maze of inscriptions across his body. I recognized him as a predator and felt something pulse from within him. I was fairly sure that made me the prey.

In that moment, while he was distracted by his burning hand, I made my move. I reached across to his wing, and pulled feathers, while pushing with all my strength to get past him. I toppled furniture behind me as I ran. When I reached the library, I pulled the lever to close the passage and screamed for Maye at the top of my lungs.

Liam

I spent my childhood bowing to my mother's every whim. As teenager, I grew a pair and rebelled against her. The last straw had been when my mother's domination over every aspect of my father's life, led to him abandoning us.

When I turned 18, I moved out and took a year off from school. At 19, I was home schooling myself to make up my last year of high school. My education began my escape from my mother. There were some members of the coven I couldn't bring myself to shun. My aunt who had taken over my dark arts training was one of them.

I had some anxiety about my mother's request involving the witch prodigy. I wasn't sure how to make someone fall in love with me; my specialty was convincing women to fall into bed with me. I wasn't anxious to try that with the Cross girl.

My mother had a skewed view of the world and the people in it. She thought that whatever she wanted was hers for the taking, but didn't understand that it was merely that way within the coven.

Most witches were born into a coven and it became their only choice. However, the Cross girl was descended from a royal line. The Cross family was known for splitting hairs where magic was concerned. They had been the founding members of both the Sacred Moon and Meadow Falls covens. This gave the Cross girl an advantage because she could choose her destiny. Her blood flowed towards two separate paths and it was her choice that would decide which vein to clamp. Once in place, it was unlikely that she could remove the clot and regain that choice.

My earlier assumptions involving the Cross girl, Savannah were wrong. My mother provided all the information I would need to insert myself into Savannah's life, but given her childhood I wasn't confident in my skills. She was raised to despise black magic. She would probably choose to be initiated into the coven who took her in. I didn't see how I could pull her away from her family within a few weeks. It would be better for her if she stayed far away from my mother's manipulations.

I reached my apartment door to find that it was unlocked, which wasn't a surprise. I opened the door to reveal the three women I enjoyed earlier that morning. They were in a similar state to the one I left them in; barely clothed and tangled in sheets on the living room floor.

That morning they begged me to stay. Considering their current activities, they obviously found adequate comfort in each other. It was a sight most men would salivate over, but had begun to bore me lately. They didn't look up, when I tossed my jacket on the couch and walked past them towards the bedroom.

I unbuttoned and tugged off my shirt as I walked into the room, and directly into the closet.

"I wasn't sure you would make it past them. I almost found them too tempting to pass up, myself." A familiar voice sounded from my room.

My shirt still off, I peeked my head around the door and smiled at the sight that greeted me. On the bed lay a seductive creature. Ordinarily, I limited my bed partners to ordinary humans, but occasionally found myself making exceptions.

Kali was one female I couldn't help giving in to. She was wild, impulsive, and a Hellhound. She wasn't the distorted perception of a Hellhound that humans had, but an actual Hellhound. Most of her race was extinct, but there were five left; five gorgeous, powerful, and terrifying females.

Death itself created the Hellhounds from tainted souls. They were the guardians of the afterlife, the takers of souls, and the dispensers of justice. In the case of a wicked soul, who escaped death, the Hellhounds would embark on the "Wild Hunt." Their punishment was far worse than the sentences death would distribute.

Hellhounds could shift at will into enormous beasts that resembled a wolf or dog, but far more terrifying. They were considered harbingers of death and could visit it upon a person merely by meeting their eyes.

"Another five minutes and I would have given up waiting for you." She said, while playing with the necklace that hung between her breasts.

"If I knew you were waiting for me, I would have been back sooner."

"Then why are you standing all the way over there? It's cold in here. I think I need you to warm me up." She purred, and turned onto her belly facing me.

I looked her over; she was wearing a black lace corset with a matching garter belt, and a g-string. Her blazing red hair hung down in a mass of waves. I cursed my slowness, and strode to the bed.

Smiling, Kali sat up and kneeled at the edge of the mattress. "Mmmm... I missed you." She said, and grabbed me by the waist band, and pulled me on top of her.

Savannah

I fidgeted in the rocking chair, waiting for Maye to return from the passageway. I shouldn't have let her go in there alone, but I couldn't bring myself to go back. The idea of it sent chills across my spine.

"Darling, there isn't anyone in there."

Maye stared at me in pity. I knew the look, because she wore it whenever she referenced my past.

"I know what I saw. It was this thing, it had wings, and..."

"Oh sweetie, I know you think you saw something. It's not that I don't believe you, I just think that it was a hallucination." She moved to brush my hair with her fingers. "The stress of being in this place has probably gotten to you and I doubt you slept well last night. It is completely normal to think you saw something that wasn't really there, under these circumstances."

I thought about Maye's logic and it made sense. If there had been something in the passageway, Maye would have seen it too. I did have heightened emotions and we did just talk about me facing my demons… Could I really have imagined it all? I felt foolish and I knew my face showed this.

"Do you want me to get the items from the room? I could call Ash and have the boys come get them."

"Yeah… I think Ash should do it. I don't want to go back there and I don't want you to hurt your back." I paused. "I'm sorry if I scared you. This place gives me the creeps. I'll be happy once it's sold and I never have to come here again."

Maye giggled; a bizarre sound coming from a robust middle aged woman. "I say that we take the rest of the afternoon and make a girl day of it." She winked.

"Oh, no. Not more shopping, please say you don't want to shop. Please, please, please…"

"I was thinking more along the lines of a spa day. What do you think? We could go see a movie after…" Her voice trailed off. I realized she was offering the girl day because it was something *she* needed, not because she felt sorry for me.

"If I must." I gave her an exaggerated sigh. "To be pampered for an entire afternoon, I shall positively die of it." Holding my hand to my forehead, I pretended to faint. I opened one eye to see Maye beaming in happiness. I would endure anything for her.

6 MAGNETIZED

Sixth Entry: Facing my Demons

Visiting my parents' estate was an experience I was glad to be done with. The more I thought about the man with wings in the passageway, the more I realized I was stupid to think it was real. Of course, my mind could make up something horrific when under that much strain.

Ash picked up the things from the passageway and everything else that I couldn't carry. He put most of it in the attic and I planned to get a better look at the collection of items soon.

I'm beginning to worry about Ash. He was cold towards me this afternoon and he has never been that way. Did I do something wrong?

Savannah

Izzy and Willow came by my house to get ready before the bonfire. That's usually how it worked out. Willows house was cramped with too many family members. Izzy lived in an apartment that was considered a two bedroom, but really her room was closer to a walk in closet.

The bonfire was little more than an annoyance on my attention radar, but was obviously socially significant to Izzy. It wasn't that she necessarily wanted to "socialize" at the bonfire, but she wanted to broadcast to the general population that her antisocial behavior was a personal choice, not a sentence to social leprosy.

I had misgivings about being around those who were not part of the coven, while this close to my ascension. I knew that the closer I was, the more dangerous I became. My gift would gradually become uncontrollable, as I approached my 16th birthday.

If my emotions became chaotic, my gift would inevitably follow. I had nightmares the bonfire would turn into a real life Carrie remake and I would star as the psychotic witch who destroys everyone in a fiery rage. I knew this was unlikely, but it didn't stop me from worrying.

I would be a landmine hidden beneath the teenage population, awaiting an unwary shadow to make a wrong step, in the unending pursuit of impressing the teenage socialites that were the cafeteria one crowd. That wrong step could result in an explosion of my power and could have seriously terrible consequences.

It was times like this that I regretted keeping my other life separate from Izzy. She wasn't a witch, but she was my friend and someone who I thought would understand.

I put the finishing touches on my makeup and stared in the mirror. Izzy and Willow were getting ready in the bedroom, but I wanted to be alone. I was feeling nervous about going out looking like this; especially when my gifts were acting up.

I groaned at my appearance. I chose to leave my hair down for once and let it dry naturally. Loose curls hung down my back with wild abandon. I rarely wore make up, but Izzy taught me some techniques. I gave my eyes the smoky gray look, added some highlights to my cheeks, and the barest amounts of pink lip-gloss. I didn't need foundation or mascara.

I wore a burgundy mini dress with a sweetheart neckline, a tapered waist, and a slightly flared skirt. The bell sleeves hung loose, and my back was completely bare down to the very bottom. I felt exposed. Izzy forced me to buy a bra that linked in front, but was backless and strapless. The cups were sticky, and I personally thought that calling it a bra was an insult to actual bras. Still, it gave me the merest sense of coverage and I was thankful for any. Izzy tried to convince me to buy a pair of strappy stilettos but I told her she was insane. Instead, I wore a pair of gray flats. I didn't need heels with my height and I wasn't sure I would be able to walk in them.

Sucking in my breath, I stepped out of the bathroom. Willow giggled on the floor pointing at Izzy, who did not look happy. Considering her outfit, I had a difficult time containing my own laughter.

"Oh. My. God!" I was trying to be nice. I really was, but I couldn't contain my laughter. Izzy, the queen of fashion or at least, gothic fashion was wearing an outfit that a clown wouldn't be caught dead wearing.

Izzy's mom had this irritating, but funny way of adjusting Izzy's clothing. She thought she was encouraging her daughter's unique sense of style, but really her creations were ridiculous. Izzy, couldn't bring herself to tell her mom that she hated the adjustments, and instead wore them. Talk about unconditional love.

"Hm. Yeah, I am pretty sure that is the worst one yet!" I shouted.

Izzy had a pained expression on her face. Her dress, which was originally beautiful, now looked like an 80's prom dress designed for a corpse. It combined gray lace, bright pink tulle, and a tie die torso.

"Please tell me, I can wear something of yours!" Izzy begged.

I immediately felt guilty when I saw the tears streaming down her cheeks. She didn't wait for my answer, but took the dress off and threw it into the backpack she brought it in.

"Yeah, but you might want to spill some paint on that dress. That way you have a future excuse not to wear it."

"Paint would be an improvement." Willow said. She then jumped up and started combing through my closet. She pulled out a pair of black shorts with suspenders attached, and a cropped top sewed to the suspenders. It was a cute outfit, which was the only reason why I had made an exception to my midriff rule.

Izzy grabbed it, shrugged, and climbed right into the outfit. The suspenders rested on the outer edges of her breasts and the shorts ended at mid thigh. The fit was entirely different on her than it was on me. The midriff looked cuter; because she had her naval pierced with a filigree black rose hanging from a small white gold chain. She looked adorable, and I knew there was no way I could wear that outfit after seeing her in it. She was made for it. Willow wore a black satin pencil skirt with a white blouse and a black vest. In short, we all looked vastly different than normal.

"You should wear a different necklace. I don't think the blue stones look right with the dress you're wearing." Willow lifted the pentacle hanging from my neck. I flinched; worried that it would burn her. It didn't really burn the winged man because he was a figment of my imagination that had been produced by massive amounts of stress.

"I like it." The truth was that even though I realized my encounter at my parents' estate was a hallucination, I couldn't bring myself to take off the necklace. In my hallucination, the necklace had protected me, hadn't it?

Ash

I spent the day avoiding Savannah at all costs. I could hear her through the walls and it was tearing me up inside to not be with her. I couldn't risk being alone with her again after I almost kissed her. What if I lost my will and gave in? It could result in the greatest sacrifice of my life, because she is the one person I could not live without. Savannah saw me as a brother, and if I wanted to keep her I would have to treat her as a brother would.

It was a relief to go to the bonfire. The group of people who went to these types of parties didn't appeal to Savannah, which made it more appealing to me.

"Hey, Ash!" Griffin piled out of a jeep with three other guys from the coven and Isis.

Most of the people at the bonfire were from school, but sometimes the older coven members came out of boredom. I sat alone by the fire. My irritability turned everyone else away. Griffin left the others and took the seat on the log next to me.

"Hey." I spoke in a monotone and looked to the side to see Griffin shift uncomfortably.

Griffin and I were raised together. We had been through some extreme circumstances, and when my parents died he understood in a way no one could expect a four year old to. Most people didn't understand our friendship and why I would want to be friends with someone so crude. However, he was different when we were alone. Savannah thought he was a jerk. I couldn't blame her, but until she came along, he was my only family besides Maye. Now Savannah superseded that relationship.

Griffin cleared his throat. "Sorry, about yesterday. I shouldn't have egged Isis on. You still mad?"

"No, not mad. It was a stupid thing to do though. It could have had some serious consequences." I looked across the fire to see Savannah climbing out of Izzy's car and was dumbstruck.

"Yeah." Griffin saw me staring across the fire and followed my line of vision to see Savannah.

"What's she doing here?" He sounded tired.

"No clue."

"Whatever. See ya." He stood suddenly and walked over to the others from the coven.

Savannah neared the bonfire and I was completely transfixed. Ordinarily, she preferred to be invisible in a gathering. It looked like she intended something entirely different tonight. She walked with her head held high and a determined gleam to her eyes.

I groaned. It was difficult enough being around her, but now every guy in the vicinity would be tempted. How could I play the over protective brother, when I was one of the hormonal guys she needed protection from?

Savannah stopped at the bonfire and waved when she saw me. That was when I began to feel the pressure in the air. My ears popped the way they do on an airplane, and my skin prickled. Aggression built until I saw what was causing my dominant nature to heighten. The feeling steadied to an even platform.

Someone stood against the dark section of the woods behind clustered groups of teens. I couldn't see his face, but he was watching Savannah. When she walked his head turned to follow. I didn't like that his eyes were stalking her. My territorial instincts were kicking into high gear, and Savannah was definitely *mine*.

Liam

I hadn't seen the Cross girl before, but my mother gave me a sock she owned as an infant. It allowed me to sense her when she was near. She had a distinct aura that was nearly as tempting as her appearance.

I came to the bonfire expecting to be bored, feigning interest in a teenage girl, who possessed gifts she didn't understand. Instead, I saw a natural beauty whose power bent around her as she moved. It was doubtful she was aware of using her gift, but I could see it.

Her gift met mine in a dance of wills. My power spun around her curling through the air. It was a game of seduction I would dominate.

Savannah's head twitched to the side and looked around. It seemed that she could sense me when I felt her push back. She did not even flinch at the use of power. It was as though her power had a mind of its own. Mine embraced her's in a waltz. I was strong and possessive. Her dance was one of grace and sensuality.

She walked towards her friends, but her body began to sway. She could feel it too, but didn't yet understand what it was.

Savannah

The feeling I experienced earlier in the kitchen was back, and making me dizzy. Did other witches feel this when they approached their ascension?

It began as a fluttering in my stomach, tingled down my spine, then warmth that built in my chest and spread to the rest of my body.

The feeling was slightly different that it had been earlier. It came in waves like the flowing of the sea over sand. If I was the sand, what was the sea?

I noticed him. He was hidden behind people and trees. His eyes were invasive and didn't flinch at my gaze. Willow and Izzy misted from my mind as I walked towards him. He had blond hair and dark eyes. He was taller than me and toned.

I walked and stopped in confusion. The feeling was stronger now and my body began to answer its call. Lips parted and my body swayed in a secret rhythm. He moved away from the trees, planting himself directly in front of me. He had met me halfway, but looked confused by his actions.

He didn't seem in control, as his hand reached out to trail along my neck towards the neckline of my dress. I didn't stop him; *couldn't* stop him. I yearned for him and when he touched me I craved him. My eyes felt weighted, while my body was magnetized.

"Who are you?" I whispered, softly. Energy pulsed between us, but halted at my voice.

The energy pulled away. Silently, I called to it. I begged it to stay and when it refused, I tried to capture it. It was an internal match that I lost.

His eyes were wide and somewhat frightened. Why was he afraid?

The expression disappeared. "Liam."

"Huh?" I couldn't process what he was saying, but I was fairly sure I just made an idiot of myself.

Smiling, he repeated his name. Then cleared his voice and said "You're from the Meadow Falls coven, right?"

He knew about witches? "How?"

His eyes lit upon the area behind me and a domineering smile gained ground on his face.

Air movement halted, sound stopped, and time stood still. A low growl filled the air behind me and I spun to see Ash's teeth barred. He took an offensive stance and pulled me behind him. His fangs showed, but I didn't think anyone besides us could see.

Liam stood straight. He didn't give ground or attempt to take it. He stared Ash in the eyes without a single flinch, but when he looked at me something exploded from Ash.

To the naked eye, they looked like two guys fighting over a girl. However, as a witch I saw something different. Ash's aura heightened to red flames and consumed Liam. In response, Liam threw up a shield of gold. While their gifts silently battled their bodies clashed.

Ash snapped his fangs at Liam, and Liam landed a blow to Ash's gut. I cried out at the sight of blood splattering to the ground. Punches flew at such a fast pace that I lost track of who threw them. Liam moved backwards and crouched defensively. I don't think they were aware of my presence any longer. Eventually, the battle moved towards the woods; away from the others.

"What's going on?" Willow whispered in my ear.

I had been so focused on the fight between Ash and Liam that I wasn't aware of Izzy and Willow's approach.

"I don't know. One minute I am talking to Liam and the next Ash is here attacking him. What should I do?" My worried stare reached for Willow's.

Izzy tugged on my arm to pull me into the woods. "One thing I know for certain, you don't get between two dogs fighting over the same piece of meat."

"Huh? First off, that comparison is unfair; they are not dogs. Secondly, they're not fighting over a piece of meat!"

I could see the fight taking place deeper in the woods, but couldn't tell if either of them was badly injured. Panic started to build in my chest and I ran forward with Izzy and Willow following. We stopped at the edge of the clearing where the battle continued.

"You're the meat." Izzy said, out of the corner of her mouth.

I turned to face Izzy's assessing stare and turned to look at Willow. Her hand covered her mouth in horror, but the look in her eyes told me that she agreed with Izzy.

"Just stay away from her!" Ash spoke before Liam kicked the back of his knee. Ash's knee buckled and he reciprocated with a flare of magic that caught Liam's shoulder in a fiery smolder.

Liam held his shoulder with a grimace, while panting from exhaustion.

"Do you have a claim to her?" Liam spoke from the opposing side of the clearing, while Ash stood. "I think she's a big girl and is smart enough to make her own decisions about who to be around. Why don't you ask her what she wants?"

Ash's face was twisted in anger until he heard the last of what Liam said. He had the wisdom to look ashamed when he stared me in the eyes.

"Ash, I was just talking to him. I've never met him before and he's right, you should trust me to make my own decisions." I felt a strong urge to wrap my arms around Ash to comfort him. The light bruising across his jaw and the blood trickling down the side of his mouth made me queasy. I couldn't bear for him to be in pain, but I didn't want him to think that I supported his actions.

"I trust you. I just..." Ash made a sound of irritation with a pained expression. He lowered his voice and said, "I didn't like it, okay? I'm sorry. I don't know why I acted so strongly. It was like I couldn't fight off the anger and it overwhelmed me. I couldn't help but give in to it."

Ash slowly approached me and reached out his hand to hold my cheek. I turned my head away at the cold touch of his fingers.

I looked up to see Liam leaning against a tree. He was bent forward slightly, as though he couldn't bear to stand straight. His right hand held his stomach and he stared directly into my eyes.

"I don't know about you guys, but I think we should get out of here. Someone might have called the cops when the saw you fighting." Willow glanced back at the trail we came through.

It made sense that we should leave. It didn't matter if the cops showed up or not. The guys looked terrible and needed to be cleaned up.

"Can one of you drive Ash home?" I ignored Ash and looked to Willow and Izzy for their agreement.

"I can drive myself." Ash's eyes blazed in anger. It was one of his most telling traits. I always knew what he was feeling by looking into his eyes.

"No, you can't. After what you did, I don't trust your judgment. You are not driving and that's final!" I crossed my arms and dared him to argue. I watched as he swallowed back his anger.

"Why don't you drive me then? You can drive my car. Besides we live in the same house."

"I'm going to take Liam home. I don't think he's in shape to drive either and I certainly don't trust you to take him home. Considering your behavior tonight, he's more likely to end up in a hospital somewhere than home."

"I don't want you alone with him." Ash whispered in my ear. "He feels wrong. I can't pinpoint it, but he's off. Please, don't go with him."

Ash gave me a pleading look that almost made me give in, but then I saw Liam and felt responsible for the pain Ash caused him. I steeled myself against the softening that Ash invoked in me and refused to give in.

After a few moments of silence, we could hear branches splinter. I had a flash of cops rushing into the clearing and handcuffing Liam and Ash.

Instead of cops, it was Griffin. He took in our group and the injuries that Ash and Liam had sustained. I watched as his eyes fixated on the bruise spreading across Ash's cheek. His teeth ground and he looked at me with an accusing stare. He blamed me for the fight. Did he think I had some mind control over Ash's actions?

"I don't mind taking him home, if that's what he wants." Izzy turned to Ash with a questioning look.

"Yes. It's what he wants." I spoke to Izzy, but stared at Ash. His eyes flared for a moment before dying down. He stared me down and finally looked at Izzy and nodded.

Willow breathed a sigh of relief, looked at me in pity, and followed to the car. Ash paused before following. When he reached the edge of the clearing, he turned to look at Liam.

"Hurt her and I will hunt you down. Got it?"

"I would never dream of it. Though it's tempting just to see you try." His bruised lip quirked in a half smile.

When Ash moved forward, Griffin grabbed his arm to pull him back.

"It's not worth it man. He's just egging you on. Let it go." Ash allowed Griffin to pull him away, but shouted back to me. "Make sure you're home at a decent hour. I don't want to have to bail him out of jail when he makes good on his promise!"

I rolled my eyes towards Liam. He remained silent as I looked him over. I wasn't particularly sure I wanted to be alone with him, but I felt that I was responsible for the situation he found himself in.

"I take it you want to drive?" He remained across the clearing.

"Do you think I just told Ash those things to sound pretty? If I let you drive then there is really no point to me seeing you home safely." I crossed my arms and attempted the stare Maye used on me whenever she thought I wasn't using common sense.

"Well princess, how do you plan to get home once you take me to my apartment? Have you thought that far?"

"Of course I have!" I turned in anger to walk quickly towards the cars. I didn't have the faintest clue how I was going to get home from his place. I still had some money left over from the shopping spree, but I had no idea if it would cover a taxi. I couldn't take his car, because then I would need to return it. Obviously, calling Ash to pick me up would be a bad idea and Izzy needed to be home before curfew.

"No clue, huh?" Liam startled me when he spoke at my shoulder.

"No clue about what?" Play dumb…just play dumb and he will let it go. That's what other teenage girls did, right?

"I'm not going to make it that easy, princess." He smiled, and jangled his keys in front of my eyes. I grabbed them and decided I was not going to point out that I only had my driver's permit.

"Stop calling me princess. Where's your car?" I stopped at the edge of the woods and looked over the assorted cars in front of me. I looked at him and back at the cars. I knew which one was his the moment I set eyes on it. Figures, that he would drive something black and sleek.

"It's the mustang."

I couldn't stop myself from snorting at the ridiculous car. Okay, not so ridiculous, because I was dying to drive it, but it was kind of cliché that *he* would own a car like that.

"Did you just snort at my car?" His brows raised in mock surprise.

"Just get in the damn car." The interior was just as divine as the exterior. Sleek with buttons I was afraid to touch, since I didn't know what they would do.

"You see that little metal thing dangling from the chain? That's the key. It's what you use to start the car…"

He was really starting to tick me off. I looked over at him and waited for him to make his next remark. *I* had the keys and there was no way I was going to drive home a pompous jerk. He could just drive himself!

"Jeez, it's like an iceberg in here! You need to lighten up, princess. I'm just teasing you."

There was that smile again. That arrogant smile he seemed to think would make everyone bow to his superiority. He was infuriating.

"If you don't stop calling me princess this car isn't going anywhere." I crossed my arms and leaned back in the seat with the car keys clenched tightly in my fist.

Liam threw up his hands in mock defeat. "Okay, okay! You win, Savannah."

When he said my name, his voice deepened to a seductive huskiness that made me shiver. I suddenly wished he would go back to calling me princess. I could deal with irritation, but I didn't want to embarrass myself because my body was seduced by the tone of his voice. Seriously, I thought that only happened in the movies. I was not one of *those* girls. Was I?

"Whatever." Then engine roared to life. "Where do you live?"

7 WITCHLINGS

Liam's apartment wasn't what I expected. From his car, I thought his apartment would be closer to a luxury condominium, but it was more of a modern bachelor pad. Ordinarily, I would not follow an infuriating male I barely knew into his apartment, but I felt compelled to see to his injuries. Maye would have been disappointed if I dropped Liam off without being completely sure he was taken care of. After all, being part of a family meant that you were partially responsible for their actions.

Witches rarely kept similar first aid kits to ordinary people, but Liam produced one from his bathroom. That surprised me. I would have offered to perform what little healing I could, but with my powers in turmoil he was better off with the first aid kit. Throughout the drive Liam continued to bait me with his remarks, which bothered me until I realized that his teasing was flirting. Flirting was a new concept to me. I tended to give people the cold shoulder and it made people keep their distance. In Liam's case, he seemed to be enjoying my annoyance and found my icy personality to be amusing.

"Why do you have a first aid kit if you are a witch?" He winced as I applied the hydrogen peroxide to his split eyebrow, and then lifted one side of his mouth to smile.

"Is there a problem with owning a kit?"

"No, it's just unusual. Wouldn't it just be easier to have another witch heal you?" I leaned in to blow on his cut to soothe the pain.

"Do you see any other witches that live with me?" He mockingly glanced around. "It's just easier to take care of my injuries myself, rather than going to my coven whenever I get a scrape."

"Oh. I guess that makes sense, but why don't you live with your coven?" A coven was like a family, but with ties that exist on a higher plane. I couldn't imagine leaving the Meadow Falls coven.

"My coven isn't like yours. My mother is the high priestess and she is more concerned with politics than she is with personal relations."

Liam

Savannah patched me up and listened to my stories about the members of my coven. It didn't take long for me to realize that she wasn't like the women I knew. Whenever I tried to tease her she pulled away. Her company was enjoyable in an awkward way. She didn't like to be touched, but had no issues with initiating the touching. She liked to be in control and seemed unused to attention. In the car she was frigid towards me, but that changed once I started talking to her as a friend. Our conversation went from forced to natural.

I managed to convince her to stay for dinner and I cooked a stir fry. She seemed genuinely surprised that I knew how to cook. I managed to find some left over ice cream for dessert. I told her that my coven was a dark one and she looked at me in horror with her mouth paused halfway through eating.

"I think I better leave." Her spoon dropped to the bowl and she stood quickly almost toppling over her chair in the process.

"What's wrong?" My hand wrapped around her upper arm. I watched as her skin blazed to burn my hand. I tore it away to find blisters spreading across my palm. Her skin faded from a fiery color to her natural ivory tone.

"Don't touch me." Her eyes were wild. "I don't like your kind. To think, I was starting to second guess my first impressions of you! I'm leaving now." She grasped the door handle and pulled, but it didn't budge. Shaking it some more she grew frustrated turning to stare at me, as if blaming me for the door being stuck.

"The door is warped. It gets stuck sometimes. What do you mean by my kind?"

After an exasperated sound escaped her lips, she turned to face me with her arms crossed. "I mean a witch like my parents. A witch who practices the dark arts."

Silence echoed off the walls, while I processed her prejudiced comment. I knew about her parents. Everyone in my coven knew about them. There were dark witches and then there were *dark* witches. Savannah's parents were the worst sort. I would rather be torn to pieces by a pack of wolves than been a victim of theirs.

I cleared my throat. "I'm not a witch like your parents. I may practice the dark arts, but I am not into killing and torturing."

When silence met my comment, I continued. "Look, you know about dark and light witches, right?" She nodded. "Okay, well I am a dark witch, but that means that I am fine with using magic for personal gain. More importantly, I believe in using my magic as protection in a fight. If some jerk attacks me, I believe that it's fine to tap into my gift to protect myself. White witches won't perform magic that would harm someone even if it means that they die. It's a matter of personal preference. Your parents on the other hand, were technically dark witches. However, my coven did not condone their actions any more than yours did."

"What do you mean my parents were a different type of dark witch?" The anger had evaporated and now Savannah looked confused.

"Take ordinary humans for example. If a saint were a witch, they would practice the whitest shade of magic. If murderers were witches, they would practice magic so dark that it would literally be the absence of color. Then there are ordinary people. Some lie, some cheat, others just go through their day and try not to hurt anyone. Those people would be white and black witches, but on the spectrum of color they would be different shades of gray."

"So what you're saying is that you are a darker gray than me?" Her brows crinkled and she relaxed against the door.

"Yes. I'm not like your parents, okay?" I moved forward to brace my arms on either side of her. She tried to avoid my stare.

"Sorry I burned you. I'm close to my ascension. It happened without me trying to." She grabbed my hand to examine it and looked up with tears in her eyes. "I don't like to hurt anyone. I…I don't want to be like them, ever." Her hair fell into her face, as she bent to kiss my palm. When she looked up she seemed embarrassed.

"Hurting me on accident does not make you like your parents. Sometimes accidents happen and with you this close to your ascension it's natural." I smoothed my thumb across her lower lip and it quivered in response. Her pupils widened. "I admire you for turning out the way you have. Had they been my parents I don't know if I would have had the strength to fight."

"Ash and Maye are the only reason I'm not like my parents, if it wasn't for them…" My pointer finger pressed against her lips to silence her.

"Ash and Maye gave you a choice. What you did with your choice was entirely up to you." I whispered the last word into her ear.

The feeling from earlier was back again. It was like a pressure building in the pit of my stomach, pushing me to merge with her. Her body language changed suddenly and I knew she could feel it too. The air around are bodies was charged like electricity and I could see our auras merge to blend together. Our senses heightened to an almost painful intensity until I touched her again. With our skin touching the pain gave way to waves of pure ecstasy. I leaned in to graze my lips against the tip of her nose and her breathing changed to a slight whimper. Her hands touched my abs and moved upwards to grasp the fabric of my shirt that lay over my chest. She pulled me closer.

Her face tipped up and I captured her lips. Her body relaxed into mine and she pulled my neck down for better access to my lips. She was inexperienced, but she kissed with a fervor that made up for that. Her lips parted and I took the chance to slip my tongue into her mouth. She gasped at the invasion, but when I kissed her more gently she began to hesitantly explore my mouth. Her tongue twisted around mine in a dance of wills and we eventually settled into a rhythm that was both hungry and sensual.

Ash

I rode home with Griffin instead of Izzy and Willow. Griffin kept quiet the whole ride and dropped me off on the street in front of the house. At first, I tried to pretend I wasn't waiting for Savannah to walk through the front door. After checking the driveway for the millionth time, I had to admit it to myself. Now, I sat in the living room with the lights low and a book in my lap.

I wasn't angry anymore. Honestly, I don't know why I lost my temper earlier. Savannah had been right, I should trust her. My instincts came alive when I saw him watching her. It was primal and an emotion I never felt before now. I was ashamed that I didn't fight it and worried that Savannah wouldn't forgive me.

Where was she? I thought she was going to take Liam to his place and then come straight home, but it was approaching midnight. My throat felt tight and I worried that I may have driven her to trust the wrong guy. There was something wrong with Liam. I hadn't lied when I told her that. Now, I couldn't stop imagining all the horrible scenarios that Savannah may be placed in.

When I wasn't worrying over Liam harming her, I was torturing myself with what other activities they might be up to. I never had to worry about Savannah with guys. She wasn't interested and they naturally sensed that enough to stay away from her. She had been different tonight. Maybe it was her ascension drawing near, but it could have been *him*.

Lights flashed in the driveway to reveal a black mustang pulling in. A closer inspection revealed that Liam was driving. I pushed my anger back at the memory of Savannah saying she wouldn't let Liam drive and forced myself to be calm. I desperately wanted to watch out the window until Savannah was safely inside. However, if she realized I was spying on her it would serve as more proof that I didn't trust her.

I walked to the entryway between the hallway and the living room to wait for Savannah. I knew Liam walked her to the door, because I could hear faint voices through it. My impatience was growing, but I forced myself to take a casual stance against the wall until she was inside. Savannah was transformed by the smile that stretched across her face, but it made me uneasy. She turned away from me to climb the stairs.

"Hey." Her back tensed at my voice, but she turned to face me with her hand clenched around the railing.

"Is there something you need?"

"I'm sorry. There is no excuse for the way I acted earlier. I was a jerk and I hope that you won't hold it against me. I may have misgivings about Liam, but I should have handled it differently."

She looked at me from the third step of the staircase and smiled hesitantly. "I'm still upset with you, but I'll come around. I do expect you to apologize to Liam too."

"I take it that means you are seeing him again?" I didn't like the sound of that.

"Yes, I think I am." She smiled and turned to go upstairs. I followed closely behind. My mind was working at a face pace to process, what it would mean if she saw Liam again and how I would react to it. The idea of her dating him made me queasy.

Savannah stopped at the entrance to her room and leaned against the door. "You want to come in? We could watch a movie? We haven't done that in a while."

There was a very good reason why we hadn't done that in a while. Lying on her bed watching a movie was not easy for me. After tonight, I didn't think it would be a good idea to refuse. I could use as many points with her as possible.

"Yea, sounds like a good idea. No girlie movies, okay?"

"Ha! After tonight, *I* get to pick the movie. I'm thinking *Titanic* or *Ever After*..."

I groaned. Three hours of *Titanic* was not appealing and Ever After wasn't much better.

"Mmmm, I'm not sure I could withstand the pain of watching either of those." I feigned a yawn, "I'm suddenly exhausted." Savannah playfully punched my arm.

"Okay, how about a romantic comedy?" I nodded and followed her into the bedroom. She put on *Made of Honor* and we curled up on her bed. Her head tucked into the crook of my arm and we relaxed into a familiar routine.

She fell asleep on my chest halfway through the movie, while I lay awake tempted by the scent of her lingering perfume. When the movie reached the last ten minutes, she startled herself awake. Sitting up she turned to glance around the room with a confused expression on her face. Her eyes lit on me and I was entranced by the expression that crossed her features.

"Ash..." The voice that escaped did not sound like *my* Savannah. She sounded like the frightened little girl she used to be. It was the sound of the lost child, who didn't believe anyone could love her. Her eyes widened and her voice pleaded, "Ash..." I couldn't bear the pain that emanated from her. It wasn't merely her voice or appearance; I could *feel* her aura calling out for me to heal her. She was back in that metal cage being forced to witness her parents sacrifice innocent after innocent. I could hear her longing, her profound need to be saved. "Ash, please..."

Her hand reached for me, while her eyes remained locked in her mental prison. I circled her wrists with my hands and pulled her to me. I meant to wrap her body with my own and offer warmth, but when I cradled her to me her cheek pressed against mine.

Her hand gripped my skin hard enough to bruise me. It was painful, but not nearly as much as what she was enduring. Every night since she came to live with us, I watched her be torn from the inside out. Her demons ate away at her every day. This was different. Lately, her nightmares had worsened and I didn't know how to banish them. I wanted to keep her safe, but I didn't know how to save her from herself.

Her tears moistened my cheeks and my heart broke at the contact. Something snapped in me then. My chest tore in two and I bridged a feeling that until now had been barricaded by as many shields as I could muster. I took her face in my hands and kissed her with the passion of a lifetime. Everything I ever felt for her was in that kiss. My need to protect her, my amazement at her respect for every living being, my love… I couldn't convey enough, but I tried. None of my emotions could overcome the amazement at the response I received. She kissed me back.

Savannah

I was restless. I fell asleep before the movie ended and woke up to a cold bed. Ash was nowhere to be seen and the window onto the terrace was wide open. I shivered and climbed out of bed to close it. My bare feet touched the floor and I felt something soft catch between my toes. I lifted my foot to find a large black feather. I massaged it between my thumb and finger, trying to figure out how it ended up in my room. Shrugging, I threw it into the trash.

The window was stuck, but it eventually gave way and allowed me to shut out the cold. The night was beautiful. The stars were more visible than usual and the moon was full. I sighed at the beauty and turned to go back to sleep. The moon shone through the glass to light up the room, but left a corner that drew the darkness from the surrounding area to create a pit.

The shadow straightened and moved to create the shape of a man, which was frightening enough. Then the wings spread to reveal the *thing* from the secret passage. A silent scream caught in my throat. I wanted to run, but then I thought of Ash and Maye. I couldn't allow this shadow to harm them. I backed away until I hit the window. I quickly opened it to climb onto the terrace. *It* followed.

I ran to the edge, but was stopped by the balustrade. I leaned over to see how far it would be if I jumped, but when I tried hands pulled me back. I fought to escape. My fingers clenched and I moved to claw its eyes out.

"S, calm down! I'm not going to hurt you!"

Tears fell before I could hold them back and I curled into a tight ball. Ash knelt and held me as I let go of my fears in his arms. He smoothed my hair away from my face and sang to calm me.

"I'm sorry." I pushed the words out between fits of crying.

"I know. I know." Ash carried me back into my room and settled me on the bed. He tucked the covers around my body, but when he tried to leave I stopped him.

"Please don't leave me. I don't want to be alone." He nodded and settled back into his position from earlier that night. I drifted to sleep in his arms.

The next morning I woke to a migraine and the smell of pancakes. On the table, beside the bed was a tray filled with a fresh breakfast. I smiled, knowing that Ash left it for me. Beside the glass of milk, I found some ibuprofen for my headache. I loved that he knew me so well. Only he would realize that I would have a migraine after nightmares.

I thought about the kiss with Liam. I wasn't sure why we had kissed. I hadn't known him long enough to develop feelings for him, but when he kissed me it felt right. I couldn't remember ever wanting to kiss anyone.

Last night had been terrifying. I was used to nightmares, but I never had issues with sleep walking and wondered at the new development. I was lucky Ash caught me. I could have ended up with a broken neck. Sighing, I tackled my breakfast.

I spent the rest of the morning resting in bed and doing homework. When I noticed that I had read the same paragraph several times over the past twenty minutes and still didn't know what it was about, I pushed the textbook away from me.

My notebook lay open next to me. I grabbed the pen and began to doodle. Thinking back to the secret passage and my waking nightmare from last night, I started to draw the *thing* and realized that I had drawn an angel with terrifying eyes and black wings. The *thing* resembled an angel, but with strange symbols across the skin and black wings. Next to the fallen angel was the box from the passage.

I tore the page from my notebook and crumpled it into a ball to toss it into the trash bin. I missed, and got up to pick the ball of paper up. Looking down into the trash, I paused at the sight of a black feather. Taking the feather in my hand, I could feel my heart beat accelerate. The feather felt *real*. I quickly sent a text to Izzy and Willow, begging them to come over.

An hour later, I sat on my bed with the feather on my lap; books lay scattered around me. The textbook I was currently staring at was about the properties of certain stones.

"Hey, sorry it took me so long." Willow startled me and I jumped to hug her.

"Wow, okay I didn't know you missed me that much!" She laughed and sat on the bed. "Um, what's with the books?" Her hand moved to pick up the feather that lay on the coverlet from when I stood up. In comparison, the feather dwarfed her hand. It was about a foot long and as wide as three fingers.

It took me some time to explain my hallucination in the passage, my dreams, and the feather. When I was finished, Willow sat in silence staring at the feather.

"Couldn't this me from one of Izzy's outfits?" She handed the feather back and I stood to place it in my dresser.

"Do you ever remember her wearing anything that had giant sized *feathers*?" I spoke forcefully, because I *needed* her to believe me.

"You said Ash put everything from the passage into the attic, right?" Willow stood and led the way towards the attic.

It took us a while to comb through the boxes, because Maye had insisted on keeping almost everything from my parents' estate. Willow got sidetracked when we found the boxes from the passageway. Once her eyes set on the journals, she was lost to me. Every half an hour I would call Izzy and leave a voicemail for her, but she still hadn't called back.

"Listen to this, your ancestor says that *he sought the dead* to learn about your lineage." Willow turned the page and blew dust from the text.

"What do you mean he sought the dead?" I grabbed the journal and tried to find the section she left off at, but Willow took it back.

"He used rituals to bring back the souls of the dead to gain knowledge."

That confused me. "Wait, I thought you needed something that represented a specific person in order to communicate with the dead?"

Willow smiled. "The blood of someone is the most significant representation of that person. Since he was their descendent, their blood was also his blood."

That was interesting. The possibilities of communicating with the first witches from your line would be amazing, but I had a feeling it would take a lifetime to communicate with *all* your ancestors.

An hour later, I was examining clothing from the passageway when Willow jumped to her feet. At first I thought that a spider must have crawled near her, but then I saw the way she was looking at the journal.

"Oh my God!" She looked at me and back at the book. "Did you know how the royal lineages were created?" I shook my head. "It says here that the first witches were Nephilim. Apparently, most of the Nephilim were whipped out of existence. However, the few who managed to refrain from destructive actions were spared. The Cross family was unique, because not only are they the descendants of Nephilim, but they also have the blood of demons running through their veins."

Willow sat on an unopened box, while I waited to hear the rest. I was descended from Nephilim? Why would a Nephilim allow their blood to mix with a demon?

It says that *"they were born to angel and man, but destined to precede the fallen unto earth. They would feed from the darkness to be born again in the light."* It then says something about how the royal lineages took part in a ritual and fed on the blood of demons.

Willow snapped the book shut and stared at me. "You know that doesn't mean anything bad, right? I mean, even if you have some demon blood in you, it doesn't make you evil."

"I know." Shaking my head, I went back to the box I had been searching through. I moved aside a silk shawl to discover the box we had been searching for. I picked it up and showed it to Willow.

Willow examined the box and had me repeat my experience in the passageway. Her brow was crinkled, which happened when she was deep in thought. She picked through some of the books we brought with us to the attic and started flipping through them. I knew this was a sign that I was dead to her until she found what she was looking for.

Now that I found the bloodstone box, I didn't have a target to look for. I pulled the box Willow had been going through and started sorting through the journals. Some of the bindings were falling to pieces, but others were perfectly preserved. I came to find that while they all looked like journals; some of them were filled with spells, rituals, and research.

I didn't spend much time looking at any specific journal, but started organizing them into piles based on their contents. At the bottom of the box, I found the newest collection. There was a journal by a man who would have been my third cousin, a great aunt, my grandmother, and my grandfather. I placed those journals in a special pile. I never considered what my other relatives would have been like, but now I was curious. Descendants of angels and demons; I wondered if any of them knew.

Lastly, a single journal remained in the box. It was more modern and in great condition. I opened it to see that the handwriting was a delicate script, which must have been a woman's. I quickly flipped through the pages and saw that the further I got in the journal, the worse the writing became. Curious, I went back to the first page and was dumbstruck, when I saw the name "Irena Cross" in large letters.

I was holding my mother's journal, which was a strange concept. I remembered my mother when she still had spurts of kindness and wondered what she had been like before she became a monster.

"Do you know what bloodstone is used for?"

Grasping the journal in my hands, I moved closer to Willow.

"I know a little. It's used to increase the power of a spell. Doesn't it also have something to do with protection?"

"Yeah, bloodstone is supposed to provide protection against demons and it also gives the user power over demons. It is also used to banish evil."

"Quartz is used for protection and containment, right?" I had heard the word demon too many times lately. I was starting to feel ill at the implications that this box had.

"S, I think this box was made to contain a demon and to protect others from it. It makes sense considering what you saw in that passage and last night…"

I held my hand up to stop her. I was beginning to feel caged in. If that box was meant to protect everyone from a demon and I unleashed it, that meant I was responsible for anyone it harmed. Oh God, what if it hurt someone I care about?

"The only thing I can't figure out is why it is interested in you. I mean, it makes sense that you would see it in the passage, but why would it follow you here?" Willow walked to me and spun me around to face her.

"I don't know! Okay? If I knew I would tell you, but I don't." My head was beginning to spin and I couldn't get enough oxygen. Willow noticed immediately and led me downstairs and back into my bedroom. I sat on the bed with my mother's journal still clenched in my fist.

"Maybe we should ask Maye about this?" Willow asked shyly.

"No!" I started to panic again. "I don't want to worry her. She'll probably just say it was a hallucination or whatever. This is something I need to figure out on my own. Besides, we don't even know if this demon is going to come back…."

Liam

"How did it go?"

I turned to find Kali sitting on the couch in my living room. She wasn't dressed to tempt, but only a saint wouldn't want to devour her. Her flaming red hair hung to her shoulders and her bright green eyes held power and wisdom. She had a knowing look, as if she were mocking me, which she likely was.

"I'm assuming you're asking about my mothers' scheme? It went fine."

"Oh, really? What's with the shiner then?" She walked to me and gently pushed the puffiness around my eye.

"That is a present from her foster brother. I think he likes me." I smiled, and wrapped my arm around her waist to pull her in closer, but she spun out of reach.

"I don't think so." She smiled coyly. "I just came to see if you need some advice, since the Cross girl is a different sort of breed than you're used to."

"I don't need advice when it comes to females." I crooked my smile at her. "You should know that."

"Ha! You don't have issues when it comes to women with no morals or in my case, women who don't have time to search for someone better." She crossed her arms and looked at me lazily.

"I was just teasing. I don't think of you in the same group as all those other women. You know that." I moved closer and tipped her chin up to look her in the eyes. "We're friends. You know that, right?" Her expression changed to a fleeting look I had never seen before and then switched back to her usual self.

"That isn't the point. I just wanted to make sure you know to take it slowly with the girl. She has been surrounded by darkness her entire life, but she still has some innocence."

"You're worried that I might corrupt her? Why do you even care?" This was a side of Kali I had never seen. She didn't normally concern herself with others and was even less likely to, when she didn't know the person.

She made an exasperated noise and shoved my chest hard enough to slam me into the opposing wall. "I do care about other people you know. Is it that difficult to believe I might have a heart?" When I stay silent with a dumbfounded expression, she continued. "Just because I was created instead of born, does not mean I don't have feelings! What I do is a job; it doesn't mean I enjoy it! Besides, I do know the Cross girl. Her parents were one of my *assignments*."

"Her parents were an assignment? You mean the Hellhounds went on a *wild hunt* to catch them? I thought the coven killed them."

Kali shook her head. "In their case, we went on the hunt to *consume* them. They were powerful witches and had a spell in place. Their bodies died, but their spirits continued to avoid death. My sisters and I hunted them down and consumed their souls. It was one of the few assignments I enjoyed." She smiled, and let loose a deafening howl. The furniture began to seizure as the wall behind Kali, appeared to crack down the center. The crack spread and the wall began to ripple. A riptide tore through the wall and swirled in a clockwise pattern. The hypnotic nature of the vortex picked up momentum, until a black hole emerged in the center. "Catch you later." Kali smiled back at me, and disappeared into the portal. There was a loud pop and the portal imploded on itself and disappeared.

I watched as her back disappeared into the portal. She must have been really bothered by our conversation, because she normally refrained from opening a portal unless it was at place of divine power. It took more energy to create a portal anywhere else.

I thought back to the implications of our conversation. It sounded as if she cared for Savannah, which was strange for a Hellhound. When one of the sisters was given an assignment it was serious business, but the sisters only went on a wild hunt for the worst cases. As one of the few mortals who knew a hellhound on a personal level, I knew what they went through.

To track down prey, the sister had to know the scent of their victim. However, a hellhound did not smell the scent of perfume or skin. They smelled the soul of their prey. To do that, the hellhound would need to immerse themselves in the memories of their prey.

When the pack went on a wild hunt, they had to immerse themselves in the entire being of that person. It is somewhat like bathing in their soul. The hellhounds would relive every action their prey took, they would feel the pain the victims felt, and the scars left behind. Kali would have taken the place of each sacrifice, she would have been immersed in the soul that offered those sacrifices, and would have endured every scar the Cross family inflicted on Savannah. I did not envy her.

8 ANGELS AND DEMONS

Savannah

It was Sunday evening and rather than finishing my homework, I was intoxicated by my mothers' journal. It was interesting to see how her writing changed as she became older. Before her ascension, she had been a normal witchling. After her ascension, she became addicted to her power.

It was strange to read about my birth and the years after. She was a completely different woman from the one I knew. She almost seemed loving, when she wrote about my birth and the first time I walked.

It was late and I could barely keep my eyes open. The words kept blurring together. I was beginning to fall asleep with the journal propped on my pillow, when my eyes caught sight of the word _demon_. As I read, I learned that my parents had researched the journals from our lineage and read about us being descended from Nephilim. They focused on how our line way unique after drinking the blood of a demon. It didn't take long for them to develop a theory about how Demonic blood mixed with Angel blood was a key ingredient to gaining power.

Once they discovered the common denominator, they began researching how to capture and angel and a demon. It didn't take long for them to realize that it was a foolish plan and was likely to get them killed. Instead, they decided to capture a *fallen angel*. Demons and fallen angels were alike and yet vastly different. Demons were truly evil creatures. However, fallen angels had once been ordinary angels, who had fallen from heaven and now possessed demonic power.

I had processed more than enough information for a single day. I wisely decided to push the journal away and felt into a comatose-like sleep. I dreamed that I was running through a forest, while being pursued by the demon. Its eyes were bright yellow and they floated towards me on the waves of darkness.

The next morning, Willow and I filled Izzy in on everything she missed the previous day. She looked worse than I felt. Her eyes were bruised and puffy and her skin had a grayish sheen to it. She claimed it was a simple cold, but I became more concerned when I saw her that afternoon walking through the halls like the living dead.

After school, the three of us went to my house and I showed them my journal. Willow scrutinized the sections I told her about, while Izzy slumped against the pillows on my bed and nodded absently at everything we said.

"Your parents were even crazier than I thought! They wanted to summon a fallen angel?" Willow leaned towards my sitting place at the edge of the bed. "Did they ever try it?"

I sighed. "I don't know. I haven't read that far yet and no you are not going to read it before me." She gave me the puppy dog look, as if it would implore me to hand over my mother journal. "I'm guessing that they did. Otherwise, why would the fallen angel have been in the box? It had to get in there somehow. My guess is that my parents put it there." I shrugged.

"Don't you want to know why the thing is stalking you?" Izzy's normally bubbly voice was now a raspy whisper. "What your parents did or didn't do doesn't really matter. It's in the past. What matters is why this demon thing showed up in your bedroom. What does it want from you?"

"Any great ideas on how to find out what it wants?" Willow and Izzy exchanged awkward looks. "That's what I thought. The only clue I have is this stupid journal. Whatever it wants is most likely related to my parents' scheme."

"Um, I have one idea." Willow ducked her head and her cheeks brightened. She didn't normally take the lead in our group and was more likely to follow our plans, not the other way around. "Well, we could take the time to read the journal, do a bunch of research, and mostly likely *still* be completely clueless. We would probably get ourselves killed in the meantime, *or...* We could summon the demon and find out what it wants on our own territory."

Willow smirked, but I could feel my courage plummet to the ground. Summon a demon and not just any demon, but a *fallen angel*? I didn't think I was that desperate.

"That is a horrible idea." Izzy voiced, before I choice say the same. "What if the demon decides to eat us or something? Are you two powerful enough to take on a freaking demon?" Izzy had a look of complete horror on her face.

"Well, no. Just listen a second, Savannah is going to go through her ascension this weekend, which means she will have full use of her power. I may not be powerful, but I can be of some help and even you can do minor magic."

"*I* can do magic?" Izzy's color came back at the tidbit of information.

"Yep, and we can put protection spells in place to confine the demon to our circle. It won't be able to touch us. We can even pull on the elements to give the circle that extra boost of power." Willow jumped to her feet and grabbed her tote. She pulled out a few books from the meadow falls library. One of them was about demons, while the others looked like spell books.

"How do we *pull on the elements*?"

Willow was busy looking for something in her books, which meant I was the designated tutor. "Everyone has an affinity for at least one element. Usually there is a specific element that is strongest. In Ash's case, he is strongest in the fire element. Willow is strongest in Earth. We are going to need to find out which elements respond to you. That way we will know which elements you can pull power from."

"How do we do that? Wouldn't I know if I could do magic?"

"Nope. The average human has no idea how to use magic and the type of books at places like Barnes and Noble do not teach the correct methods." Izzy nodded, while the crease that resided on her forehead gained ground.

"Tonight, I'll do some research on how to summon a demon safely. Can you work with Izzy to find out which elements respond to her?" Willow pushed her books back in her bag, and stood impatiently.

"Yeah, I'll work with Izzy. I still don't think I like this idea though."

Willow left and Izzy soon followed. She was too exhausted to do anything else today and I completely understood. That night I went to read my mother's journal, when Ash came into my room. His face was dominated by an irritated expression he rarely used.

"When are we going to talk about the other night?" His tone was much lower than normal and I could see he was restraining anger.

"The sleepwalking? I didn't think we needed to. I mean, there isn't really anything we can do about it. Thank you for stopping me from leaping to my death." I laughed. "That could have been awkward."

He sighed. "That's not the part of the night I want to talk about and you know it." When I stared in confusion, he moved forward to stand in front of my bed. He leaned over and placed one hand on the footboard of the bed and the other around the pole.

"You're going to stay in denial then?"

"Denial, about what? Stop being cryptic and just tell me what you mean!" I couldn't figure out what he was talking about. I racked my mind thinking about past few nights and the only things I could think of were the fight with Liam and my sleepwalking.

"The kiss." He growled more than spoke.

My mouth widened in surprise. "How did you find out that Liam kissed me? Did I talk in my sleep or something?"

"He what?" Ashes eyes blazed until they looked like fire pits and his hands tightened on the bedpost.

"Oh, you didn't know? That what kiss are you talking about?"

"Ours." If I was shocked before, I was now astounded.

"We haven't kissed." My hands began to lightly shake when I remembered my dream from the other night. It was right smack in the middle between my nightly reminder of my past and the visit from the demon.

"We kissed the other night when you woke up from your nightmare." He blew air out and his eyes lightened. His hand brushed through his hair and a short laugh escaped his lip. "Figures. I spend all this time fighting my need to kiss you and when I finally give in, you don't even remember!" He moved backwards to sit in the chair near my desk. He leaned his elbows on his knees and covered his face with his hands.

My heart broke. I thought the kiss had been a dream and now I find out I really kissed Ash. I wasn't certain how I felt about it, but I could see that he was shaken. I moved forward, knelt down, and pulled his hands from his face.

"I thought it was a dream. I'm sorry."

"Don't worry about it. It's my own stupid fault." He stood suddenly and almost knocked me over in the process. I darted towards the door and flung it open.

I followed quickly behind him. "Ash just listen to me. It's okay. I'm not angry and it's my fault too."

He stopped suddenly on the stairs and turned to face me. His crimson eyes settled on mine and I saw that the veins surrounding his eyes were blazing red. He wasn't angry; he was furious.

"Your fault too, huh? So, why is it okay for you to kiss me in your dreams, but not when you're awake?" His fangs lengthened, which only occurred when he was threatened or the one doing the threatening.

"That's not what I meant. I only meant that you kissed me and I kissed you back. I just didn't want you to be angry with yourself." I tried to touch his face, but he grabbed my wrist in an iron grip.

"Yes, you did. Why did you?" His smile turned mocking.

"Why did I kiss you back?" How was I supposed to answer that? I started panicking.

He used his grip on my wrist to pull me down the steps, until I was on the step before him. "I don't know. I was scared and I *needed* you."

"You needed me? Did you need Liam too? Or are you just going to start making a habit of kissing all the men in your life?"

That pulled me back. I was shocked and hurt by his accusation. However, I was mostly horrified by the realization that Ash was pulling away from me. I could see the connection between us shattering. It was a bridge I relied on ever since I came to live with him and Maye. I knew I didn't make it easy for people in my life. Ash had always been my safety net. He made me feel safe and the natural bond between us saved my life. He was the one person I could not live without.

"It's not like that. I don't know what is happening between me and Liam. What happened between me and you was different." Ash let go of my wrist and turned to leave. "No, don't go!" Tears welled in my eyes and began to fall. Ash looked up to see them and his face drastically altered.

He moved back to his previous position and tilted my chin to brush away my tears. "That's not fair. You know I can't stand to see you cry." His voice became a soft melody.

"I love you. I don't want to lose you." I grabbed his face and pulled it to mine. He tried to pull away from my kiss, but I protested. "Let me try." His original protest evaporated at the touch of my lips. He ground his to mine and turned to push my back against the wall.

I had issues with claustrophobia, but with Ash, I was fine. He melded his body to mine and I pushed to be closer still. Feelings I never acknowledged came to the surface to break free. A low growl came from deep in his chest and he grasped my thighs to pull me higher. I wrapped my legs around his waist and kissed harder. I moaned, and he stilled.

I opened my eyes to see him staring at me. "Are you kissing me because you want to or because you're afraid you'll lose me?"

My mind was foggy and it took a few minutes to process what he asked. During that time, Ash lowered me to the ground and let go of my thighs. He put some distance between us. "Well?"

"I don't know. I mean, I enjoy kissing you, but I never really thought about you in that way before. I didn't know it was an option."

He groaned. "Okay, well now you know." He smiled, and leaned towards my face. Instinctively, I raised my face to meet his kiss, but he moved away to kiss my forehead. "Let me know when you figure out what you want." He pushed away from the wall and jogged down the steps.

I stood in place and attempted to evaluate my feelings. Confusion didn't even begin to weigh on how I felt in that moment. I wanted to run after him and make him finish what he started, but then I thought about my kiss with Liam. What was wrong with me? Why did I keep kissing people and who did I want to keep kissing?

Liam

It wasn't difficult to locate Savannah's aura, but it was surprising to find her in a bookstore designated for witches who participate in the dark arts. Most pagan stores were owned by humans and contained spell books that would never work. However, the stores owned by witches tended to have books by real witches. On occasion, a store would be designated for ordinary humans, but would have a back room or a basement for _real_ witches. The Black Raven was the type of pagan store that masqueraded as an ordinary store. Inside it contained spell books that were as useful as a magic wand. However, behind the desk was a hallway that led to the actual store. It contained everything a practicing witch would need and was dominated by books on the dark arts.

I found Savannah sandwiched between bookcases designated for demonic spells and one for vengeance. I briefly wondered which of the two she favored when I saw her move towards the section about demons.

"Did I miss something? When did you go from despising the dark arts to shopping in a store dedicated to it?" Her startled reaction was rewarding.

Savannah smoothed her hair away from her face, which was a feminine trait that announced that she cared what I thought of how she looked.

"Um, hi. I couldn't find what I am looking for at my covens' library." She shuffled her feet and avoided looking at me.

"Why are you looking for a book on demons? Isn't that a little out of your league, princess?"

"I was reading my mothers' journal and discovered that the royal lineages are descended from Nephilim, but that the Cross family also fed on the blood of demons." She shrugged. "I got curious."

I could feel that she was holding something back, but it was never a good idea to push someone who was standing on a cliff. "You learned about that, huh?"

She blinked in confusion. "You knew?"

I laughed. "Of course, I knew. My whole coven knows. The Cross family wasn't just part of the Meadow falls coven. The Cross family was the founding family of the Sacred Moon coven too." Her brow furrowed. "Sacred Moon is my coven."

"Oh. How come my coven never told me then?"

"I would guess that the Cross family never told them. It's not exactly something they would be accepting of." She nodded absently and looked down at the book in her hand.

"If you want to know more about it, you should talk to the elders in my coven. They could tell you anything you want to know. They could tell you more about your parents too." Savannah nibbled on her lower lip, while she considered my offer.

"How much do they know about my parents?"

"After they left the Meadow falls coven, your parents joined mine. When my coven discovered some of your parents' intentions, they were removed from our coven. You were born while your parents were still a part of the Sacred Moon coven." That startled her.

I pulled the book from her grip and paged through it to see what she was researching. The book detailed information about fallen angels and how demons could increase a witch's power.

"Are you curious about fallen angels or increasing your power, princess?" I raised my eyebrows and she rolled her eyes.

"Nice." She attempted to grab the book back, but I held it out of her reach.

"You want the book and I want an answer. Care for a compromise?" I rested against the bookcase with the book held high over my head.

Savannah moved forward with her eyes locked on mine. "Well, I don't know." She leaned her body into my chest. "What type of compromise were you thinking of?" She smiled, tilted her face, and when I leaned in to kiss her, she grabbed the book and danced away. "On second thought, I don't think a compromise is in order."

"Proud of yourself, princess? Using sexual wiles on me to get what you want." I sighed. "That's typical of a woman."

"Hey!" She smacked my arm with her book and looked at me shyly. "Do you really think that your coven could tell me more about my parents?"

It didn't take long to convince Savannah to meet with my coven. I waited while she purchased her book, and she rode with me in my car to the estate where the elders lived with my mother. It was a generous estate. The main house was a miniature model of a lord's estate from England with an adjoined barn that seemed out of place.

Savannah gazed around in wonder at the inside of the hall. "This is where you grew up?"

I followed as Savannah walked from room to room in amazement. When she neared the study, she stopped at the sound of voices from within. From the tones, I knew my mother was one of the parties inside and I guessed from the other voices that a handful of the elders were arguing with her.

"Don't worry Princess, it's just my mother." I walked in front of Savannah and opened the door. "I see you're up to your usual; nagging everyone in sight. Is there any way I can convince you to take it easy on poor Savannah's ears?"

My mother turned at the mention of Savannah and her face brightened. She exchanged a proud look with me and hurried over to take Savannah's hands. "I have heard so much about you! My son won't stop talking about how wonderful you are!" She smiled.

"You got all that, from me talking about the little minx being immune to my charms?" I winked at Savannah and walked over to the others.

I introduced Savannah to the members of the coven. My mother managed to convince Savannah to stay for dinner and spent the entire time trying to charm her. It seemed to be working, because Savannah's color brightened as the day wore on. After dinner, the elders left to pursue their own activities and my mother motioned for Savannah and me to follow her back to the study.

"My son tells me you have some questions."

My mother sat in the only chair, while Savannah sat on the love seat. I didn't want to make Savannah uncomfortable and choose to stand near the fireplace. Silently, I allowed Savannah to lead the conversation.

"Yes, I recently found out that I have the blood of angels and demons in my veins. Is that true?"

"I'm not sure what answer you would like, but yes it's true." My mother leaned back in her chair to study Savannah's face. "I suppose you hoped it wasn't true?" Savannah nodded. "In any case, I don't see why it matters. All it means is that your line is extremely powerful. It doesn't mean you're demonic or angelic. You are a witch, pure and simple."

"Why would they have chosen to feed on the blood of demons?"

My mother snorted. "Why would your parents or why did your ancestors?"

Savannah gave my mother and me a startled look. "You knew about my parents plan?"

"That's what you really wanted to ask about, isn't it?" She was silent for a moment, and then turned to me. "Liam, I think that we are going to need some refreshments if we are going to have this chat. Could you see to it?"

I walked from the room in a daze. When I came back, it was to find my mother telling Savannah about her infancy.

"I was there the night you were born. Your mother was so happy. She cradled you and I could see in her face that you were the most important thing to her."

"I find that hard to believe. The mother I knew did not care about me." Savannah looked up at my approach and her face reddened.

"That only changed when they began to pursue their plans to gain power. Magic can be like any other drug. The more you have, the more you crave until nothing can sate your craving and you're willing to give up anything, to have more of it. Your mother loved you, but that love deteriorated in the face of her addiction."

The housekeeper came in with a tray of cookies and tea. She set the tray on the coffee table and handed a cup of tea to Savannah and my mother. Savannah grabbed a cookie and nibbled on it absently.

"Can we not talk about her? Could we just talk about their plans for the demon?"

"Of course, but I don't know very much about that. When we learned that your parents planned to summon a demon, capture it, and increase their power... Let's just say we weren't too keen on their plan and removed them from influencing our young."

After that, my mother told Savannah embarrassing stories about my childhood and Savannah spent most of the evening laughing, which I was grateful for. We left my mother and I drove Savannah home. I pulled into the driveway and turned to Savannah.

"Is there any way I could convince you to go out with me again? Do something that doesn't involve frustrating family members or demons?"

Savannah reached into her bag, scribbled on a paper, and handed me her phone number. "That's my cell. Give me a call and I'll give you an answer." Her cheeks reddened.

"Is this a compromise?" I laughed, and tugged on a stray hair that was hanging in her face. "Alright Princess, I'll give you a call, but you have to promise to answer."

"A counter offer… I like it. I promise to answer or to at least call back, okay?"

She climbed out of the car and made her way towards the house. A panicked feeling built in my chest and before I knew it, I was out of my car and jogging to her. She turned when she heard my approach. "I forgot."

"Forgot what?" She leaned forward, waiting for my answer.

"This." I grasped her waist and pulled her into my body to claim her mouth. She started to speak, but my lips silenced her. It was a chaster kiss than I was used to, but I was aware of her house behind her. If her guardian was inside, I didn't want Savannah to feel any embarrassment at trying to explain the kiss. I pulled away to see a surprised expression cross her face and watched as she touched her lips.

"Oh."

"See you later, Princess." I got in my car and drove home.

Ash

I looked out the window when the car pulled into the drive. I thought it was Maye, but I watched as Liam kissed Savannah. I wanted to rage at the touch, but turned towards the kitchen and forced myself to heat up a slice of apple pie. I took my anger out on the it as I forked eat bite.

A few minutes later, Savannah came into the kitchen and hesitantly approached. "Hey."

I looked up with a bite in my mouth and nodded. She walked forward, opened a drawer, and pulled a fork out. She came close and speared a piece of the pie to eat. I watched her, silently.

"I ran into Liam at the bookstore today." She didn't look at me as she said this. My hand tightened on the fork. "He brought me to see his mother and when he dropped me off, he kissed me."

"You're telling me this why?"

Savannah looked up and shrugged. "I didn't want you to think I was hiding it from you."

"Did you want him to kiss you?" I regretted the question the moment I asked it.

"I don't know." She moved to put her fork in the sink and turned to look back at me.

"It seems like you don't know a lot of things lately. Like I said before, let me know when you figure it out." I pushed the empty plate towards the sink and moved to leave the kitchen.

"Ash, he asked me to go on a date. Should I go?" I paused at her question, but I refused to turn to look at her.

"Do what you want. It's not up to me." I walked away and stayed in my room the rest of the night.

The next day I managed to avoid her at school and I went out with Griffin that afternoon. I came home to find Maye in the living room.

"I don't know what is going on between the two of you and I don't want to." She came forward to kiss my cheek. "She came home this afternoon and announced she was going on a date since you don't seem to care one way or another. She's been in her room trying on every outfit under the sun. Did you really tell her you don't care if she goes on a date?" I nodded.

"Well, then I have to tell you that was the most asinine thing you have ever said. We both know you care and once you see what she is wearing on this date, I have a feeling you are going to care even more."

"Why? What exactly is she wearing?" Maye gave me a knowing smile and left the room.

I hurried upstairs and didn't pause to knock before entering Savannah's room. I stopped short when I saw what she was wearing. Her dress looked like a satin slip with flimsy straps that would break if tugged the wrong way. Her hair was loosely piled on her head with curly strands hanging down.

Savannah turned to face me with a daring smile. She wanted me to notice the way she looked. I could see in her expression that she expected a battle and knew she wanted one. I swallowed back my fury and smiled back at her.

"You look nice. Where are you going?"

Her smile faltered, and she gave me a sly look. "I have a date with Liam. Do you think this is too revealing?" She spun in a circle to give me the full effect of her dress.

I shrugged. "It looks fine to me."

Savannah's face changed into a look of anger. She grabbed her hair brush from the dresser and threw it at me. I ducked into the hall laughing. She sounded agitated as she slammed the door in my face. Although, I didn't want her going out with Liam and I definitely did not want her going on a date dressed the way she was, I enjoyed her reaction. I feigned disinterest, but was secretly thrilled that it bothered her.

Savannah

I wanted to scream and tear apart my room. I would never understand men. One minute, Ash is jealous enough to pummel a guy I was talking to, and now he was encouraging me to go on a date dressed in lingerie? What was wrong with us?

I didn't know why I went out of my way to get a reaction out of Ash, but I knew it wasn't my normal behavior. Maybe all those kisses were beginning to go to my head. I looked down at my outfit and groaned. I was counting on Ash making a big deal of it. I never really intended to wear it out of the house. I felt naked and I wasn't sure that feeling would send the right message to Liam. Now, if I didn't wear the skimpy outfit, Ash would know I only wore it to bother him.

The door bell rang and my stomach churned. I thought about my kiss with Liam and then immediately thought of Ash. I didn't know which one I wanted and wasn't even sure my emotions were reliable right now. It was like my hormones were raging out of control and Liam and Ash were the unfortunate bystanders, who were caught in the storm.

I knew I shouldn't even be thinking about dating with the whole demon mess going on. However, my birthday was this weekend and I thought for once, I deserved to have a small piece of my world be *my* choice. My entire life I had been swept away on everyone else's wave and now I wanted to ride my own.

That evening, Liam was a gentleman and choose not to mention by risqué outfit. Although, I did notice that his eyebrows had risen and he hid a smirk. My date with Liam went smoothly, but I was disappointed that Ash didn't come to see me off. Liam brought me to the movies and straight home since Maye warned him I had a curfew. When I got home, Liam walked me to the door. When he leaned in to give me a kiss, Maye opened the door with a sour look and dismissed him.

"Maye, what was that for?" She pulled me away from the door by holding onto my upper arm.

"Isn't he a little old for you, darling?" She sounded like she normally did, but her eyes were like steel.

"No, he isn't. Besides, age shouldn't matter. He's nice and he makes me laugh. Plus, he's not afraid to flirt with me. I don't see what the problem is; you didn't have a problem with him when we left. What changed?"

She walked into the living room without looking back. "Maye!" I angrily followed her into the room, but calmed when I saw Josephine sitting on the sofa. The room smelled of Frankincense and Myrrh, which told me that Josephine had one of her visions and it wasn't a good one.

"Aunt Josephine, what's wrong?" I rushed to her, knelt on the ground in front of her, and took her hands in mine. Her hands were shaking and ice cold.

"Oh dear, I don't mean to worry you. I'm sure it's nothing." She patted my hands and looked at Maye.

Josephine was a close friend of Maye's, but was at least ten years her senior. She was on the elder council and a prominent psychic in the witch community. Witches traveled across the world for her to read their cards. She was strong with divination tools, such as tarot cards, runes, and reading tea leaves. However, she was more potent when a vision overcame her without provocation.

When Josephine was taken by a vision, she was often left weak afterwards. I worried for her. As she aged, the visions took more out of her, but there was nothing she could do to stop them. Josephine saw them as a divine gift that should be cherished.

"What did you see?" I moved to sit next to her and pulled the blanket from the back of the sofa to wrap around her frail body. She took it with a thank you.

"It wasn't very clear, child."

"Josephine, just tell Savannah what you saw." Maye's voice was laced with irritation.

"I will. I will, just give me some room to breathe." She waved her hand at Maye and turned to face me. "My visions aren't as clear as they once were. It's rather like wearing prescription glasses when you don't need them. All blurs."

"Just tell me what you could make out. You're here, you must have thought it was important." I spoke softly the way I would to a wounded animal or frightened child.

"I was watching television at home, when it happened. I fell against the cushions. Thank goodness I wasn't standing." She coughed into her palm and cleared her throat. "I saw that boy and Ash, there was so much darkness." She grabbed my wrists with all the intensity of her words. "You and your friends are surrounded by death. You need to remove yourself from your current path or death will come." Tears flooded her eyes and her body slumped into a deep sleep.

"She's exhausted. You don't know what it took for her to remain awake long enough to talk to you." Maye moved forward and ushered me away to put Josephine's legs onto the couch and covered her with another blanket.

"Why didn't you call me?"

"She wouldn't let me. This was your first date and neither of us wanted to ruin it for you."

"What makes you think that Liam is the cause of this darkness? What if I am the cause?" I thought of the demon and knew Liam wasn't the one who was bringing evil into this community.

"Liam is new in your life and has set you on a new course. It makes sense that she would have this vision when he comes into your life. I just want to protect you. I can't tell you who to date, but I want you to be careful." She kissed me on the cheek and walked towards her bedroom.

I wanted to go after her, to tell her everything, and for her to tell me it would be okay. Josephine's vision was confirmation that the demon was not going away. My ascension couldn't come soon enough. I needed the power to protect my loved ones and I would not allow them to be harmed. If I had to raise hell to protect them, I would.

9 ASCENSION

After school the next day, Izzy came to my house. I gathered everything I would need to discover her elemental affinity and we walked to my covens circle. Izzy stood awkwardly and waited while I lit the candles placed on each boulder.

I was surprised by Izzy's acceptance of this part of my life. Willow and I kept Izzy separate from the world of magic, but now I was actively carrying her into it. She stepped through the shield that bars humans from our world. Her eyes had been opened and I vaguely wondered if she would regret it.

"What do you need me to do?"

"Come here." Izzy stepped fully into the circle and sat on the cloth placed on the ground. I sat across from her.

"There are five elements; earth, air, fire, water, and spirit. Most witches excel at one affinity, but are proficient in all of them. In the case of someone who isn't a witch, they can affect the elements a bit. Usually a non-witch will only have a single element that barely responds to him or her."

"If it's barely going to respond to me, what's the point in helping? Wouldn't you guys be just as well off without me?"

"Um... not really. Even though you aren't a witch, you strengthen the circle. Look at it this way; you know the game *Light as a Feather, Stiff as a Board*?" She nodded. "If a single person tried to use their fingertips to lift someone, it wouldn't work. The more people who join in the game, the more likely they will succeed at lifting the person."

"Great, so you guys need my fingertips." She smiled. "How do we figure out which element is my ticket to taking over the world?"

I laughed, took objects from my backpack and placed them in front of Izzy. I placed a candle, chalice, a bowl filled with dirt and a hidden seed, and a feather.

I motioned to the object between us. "Okay, each of these objects represents one of the elements. Now…"

"Wait, there are only four objects. What about the fifth?"

"The fifth element is spirit, which is more of a metaphorical element. You don't usually use an object for that element. However, if you were religious I would suggest a symbol of your religion." I grabbed a bottle of water from my bag and poured it into the chalice.

"Oh."

"Alright, I'm going to test you the way witches normally test their children. First, I want to show you what it will look like when the element responds to you." I was an expert at directing the elements. Simultaneously, I lit the candle, caused the water in the chalice to spin like a whirlpool, ca small bud to grow within the bowl, and made the feather float.

"Oh my God, that is so cool!"

I let go of my control and the elements reverted to their inert state. "Now, since it would take too long to teach you to do this on your own. I am going to merge our minds so that I can pull on your power and show you how to direct it. If you close your eyes it's better, because you won't be distracted."

Izzy nodded and closed her eyes. I tuned my inner self to focus on my surroundings. I reached out to touch the life forces nearby. Tiny specks of energy flittered, but I was focused on the bright beacon within my circle. My aura enveloped me with a silver sheen. I hesitantly directed a small portion of it to reach out towards Izzy. The silvery strand connected with Izzy's bright orange aura to create a bridge between us.

Izzy gasped at the bond, but she didn't fight it. The bridge between our auras sparked with electricity, while it strengthened. Concentrating, I allowed my conscious to merge with hers and led her to the pathways within her. She became a maze of intricate paths, but I turned her towards concentrating on the ones that led outside of her body.

I guided Izzy to sing her energy into a spun web, which expanded into delicate strands she could pluck and project towards the objects in front of her. Through those strands, she would be able to manipulate the objects.

Silently, I encouraged her to direct her will, which would cause the element to respond. I let go of the reins and separated our auras. Watching her with my eyes, I could sense her struggle to use the barest amounts of magic. The objects didn't move, flutter, or spin; they simply *were*.

I was about to tell Izzy to pull back, when the feather twitched on a breeze and floated in the air. Izzy opened lost concentration when she opened her eyes. The feather plummeted to the ground, but we were done. The element that responded to her was air. That was all we needed to know.

The next few days went by in a whirlwind. Willow prepared the ritual we would use to summon the demon, Izzy practiced manipulating air to affect the world around her, and I stayed home from school. My ascension was close and it felt like it was taking over my life.

My hormones were out of control. Each time I saw Liam, I felt an invisible pull that was harder to ignore. Ash deliberately avoided me and his easy acceptance of mine and Liam's growing relationship bothered me. Ash hadn't tried to kiss me again, but at night when I wasn't having nightmares about the demon, I dreamt of his kiss on the stairwell.

The evening before my ascension Izzy and Willow came over. Their visit was meant to cheer me up, but it only worsened my discomfort when they came with bad news. Jessica, a girl who I had calculus with, died in her sleep the night before. The doctors couldn't figure out what caused her death, but she had been weakening over the past week and a half. If that news wasn't horrible enough, Willow came to my home with a theory.

Willow's research turned up some interesting information about demons gaining power. Her theory was that the demon was trapped in the bloodstone box, long enough to weaken him, and now he needed to resort to stealing the life force of others. Humans were easier prey than witches, which is why Willow though he killed Jessica.

"Willow, I love you, but I think you are jumping to conclusions. Why would his first victim occur now? Wouldn't he have done this sooner?" Willow nodded at Izzy's logic.

"I guess so. I've been reading about demons too much. I think they are rotting my brain." Willow sat on the bed, next to me, and across from Izzy.

"We can't have that! You have the best brain in our trio! If yours goes, who is going to keep us from doing something stupidly dangerous?" I nudged Willow and the three of us settled in to a girl's night filled with movies, popcorn, and a mini spell to appease Izzy.

Izzy watched the movie, *The Craft* the night before and got it in her head that changing her hair or eye color would be a fun activity. Willow and I schemed, and when Izzy looked in the mirror, she stood in horror at the spotted leopard print hair on her head.

"Oh my God! This is so not cool! Turn it back!" She threw her pillow at Willow, while I laughed so hard my abs became sore.

"Okay, come here. We'll fix it." Izzy hesitantly came forward with a distrustful expression. When we were finished, she no longer had leopard print or her normal dishwater blonde shade, but instead she was a gorgeous platinum blonde.

Izzy wanted all of us to change something about our appearance, and giving into her excitement, we agreed. Willow made her hair curly and added a red tint to her chestnut brown shade. I was hesitant when my turn came. I knew it was merely play and that I could revert back to my normal appearance at any time, but I had difficulty accepting myself as it was. If I changed my appearance, would I ever want to change back? Instead of following my friend's examples, I choose to add something rather than alter myself.

"Done!" I smiled at them, while they examined my face, hair, and skin for my transformation.

"You didn't change a thing!" "Did you forget how to do it?" They spoke at once and I laughed.

Standing up, I lifted my shirt to show them the new addition to my naval.

"You pierced your naval! Why didn't I think of that?" Izzy poked at the miniature cross and pentacle hanging from my naval. "Isn't it a little weird to put those two together? I mean, a cross and pentacle are completely different religions."

Shaking my head, I explained. "The pentacle stands for what I am and the cross stands for who I am." I winked. "Besides, they may be two separate religions, but they have a lot of the same beliefs and morals. I don't see anything wrong with either. Plus, that's not the only thing I changed." I let go of my shirt and turned around. Pulling my hair over my shoulder, I showed them the tattoo between my shoulder blades.

The tattoo was the physical representation that demonstrated my acceptance of my lineage. It was a tattoo of wings with black and white feathers. I couldn't hide who I was. When I went through my ascension tomorrow, I wanted to believe in myself and be proud of the blood in my veins.

Izzy and Willow went home early the next morning, while I prepared for my ascension. Maye performed a cleansing ceremony to purify me, which included using incense to banish negativity and body oils to lock in my natural essence. Ash brought me a lilac dress. The skirt of the gown fell to the floor, but the slightest brush of air would bring about a romantic elegance, while the dress floated on the wind. It was the most beautiful gown I had ever seen.

Willow came over later that afternoon with the elders. While they created a circle around me, Willow painted inscriptions across my exposed skin. The inscriptions were the most important aspect of the pre-ceremonial activities. Painting the inscriptions was one of the highest honors a witch could bestow on another.

Willow used an instrument, which resembled a calligraphy pen to paint inscriptions in silver, blue, and purple. She would paint six main symbols connected by scrollwork. Willow could work more inscriptions into the scrollwork, as personal gift from her to me. The symbols on my skin would represent the many cultures witches descended from. The symbols on the top of each foot would represent protection and power. The ones on my hands would be for life and transformation. The symbol on my head would represent wisdom, but the inscription on my chest was the most important, because it represented the five elements.

Once Willow was finished applying the script to my skin, she took a white robe etched in silver and placed it on my shoulders. It was soft against my skin. We waited for the elders to close the circle before stepping out. I waited in the hallway, while everyone left the house to prepare for the ceremony.

I turned to see Ash approach me. I expected his usual coldness, but instead he gave me a warm smile. "Don't worry, you'll be fine."

How did he always know the right thing to say? "I don't feel fine. I'm scared. Ash, what if the power is too much and I turn out like my parents?"

His moved forward and used the tip of his finger to brush against my neck. "You could never be like them. Have faith; I have faith in you." He leaned forward and brushed a delicate kiss to my lips. I pulled him forward and kissed him deeper.

"Promise me. Promise me, that if I turn out like them, you'll take care of me the way the coven took care of them." I searched his eyes, but they remained warm.

"I promise, but only because you will never be anyone other than yourself. Despite the evil you have encountered you remained pure. I know you believe they tainted you, but they never did. You are the most loyal and caring person I know. You put everyone else before you and ask for nothing in return. You soul is a star that blazes to warm those around you. You guide them towards the light and make them want to be a better version of themselves. You're a beacon for us to follow and you will never lead anyone off course, because you will remain on the honorable path you have always chosen. I love you and I'm telling you that you have nothing to worry about."

My heart flipped and a tear slid from my eye. "You're going to make me mess up all of Willows work." I laughed awkwardly, while he brushed the tear from my cheek. Ash walked around me, but turned back to deposit a kiss on my nape. I leaned back into him and he wrapped his arms around my middle. "Thank you." I whispered and he left.

When I walked into the circle, it was mere minutes until the 16th anniversary of the moment I was born. I stood in the center, surrounded by the Meadows Fall coven and their sister covens. In front of each of the five boulders, were five people I chose to represent each element: Willow for earth, Alice, who was Willow's mother for air, Ash for fire, Maye for water, and Josephine for spirit. They would ground me during my ascension.

I brushed my hood back from my face to reveal the delicate scrollwork and symbol for wisdom that Willow had painted. I faced Josephine to await the inevitable. I was terrified and hoped no one could see my hands shake. I knew what to expect; Maye spent years preparing me for this, but hearing about it and going through it were two separate things.

The joined members began to sing a high pitched song in Gaelic. It was a song filled with hope, love, and the acceptance of change. Their voices were melodic and calmed my anxiety. I drifted into a waking sleep; until my skin tingled and I opened my eyes to see a cone emerge from the coven. It was a cone of power and would serve as protection from outside influences.

My ascension tore into me suddenly. The cone eclipsed the world around me in an icy mist. I screamed; begging someone, anyone to hear my pleas, but my voice had been extinguished and left me with a slight wheeze from what little oxygen I had. I could glimpse the field of energy, as it shrank through the safety of my circle to envelop me in a blazing grip. I was alone; unbearably separated from my haven.

The cone shuttered, as though it were pulling against an invisible force that refused to allow it purchase. It began to fold into my physical self by plying my skin and sinking through my pores, nourishing its hunger on my soul. It burrowed through my barriers, until it found my core and coiled around my essence. I was consumed; each of my senses extended to their limits.

I was no longer *me*; my energy merged with everyone and everything around me. The oxygen I had been deprived, exerted pressure and dug its way into my chest. The world blazed brighter, as if taking its own breath. My feet became the roots that ground the trees; my hands were leaves that extended towards the sky; my skin was each and every member of the Meadow Falls coven. Here there were no secrets; here we were one. Being able to sense my coven and hear their voices once more, calmed me.

The covens magic pulsed into one purpose; one conscious goal, to merge my essence with my inner power, while building a bridge to my mental self. My power was held within me. Until now, I had been unaware of the electric blue fire at my core. My youth had protected me from irresponsible use of my power, but now it would weigh me down with each choice I made. I would be confronted by temptation to use my powers for personal gain; it was in my blood. My parents had proven that to me; I had seen what unlimited power could do to a person.

The pain came in waves. At first, I felt miniature pin pricks against my temples, but then my skin felt like it was being scraped raw by sandpaper. I could feel each layer of skin burn away. The small ball of energy within me had grown to the size of a softball. I could feel the worry emanating from the coven. I knew that it wasn't normal for my power to increase to the extent. It shouldn't be this intense; this overwhelming, and yet it was. It strained against the chains that bound it within me and raged when it could not be freed.

Confined to my petite frame, the power was enraged and pulled against my taut skin. Growing bolder, it tore through to lay flat against the outer edge. It solidified and lengthened to mold itself to my frame and contained me in a transparent cocoon.

My fingers flexed against the waxy surface, while I panicked. I was cut off from my coven now; their thoughts distant echoes. Concern showed on their faces, as I fell onto my side; convulsing within my cocoon. A seizure racked my body, while I blended into the agony. I was going to die; the old saying was true, children do pay for the crimes of their parents. I was going to be exhibit A in that time old trial.

Ash

I desperately wanted to go to Savannah, but I knew it would be foolish. Every member of the coven needed to remain in place or Savannah's life would be in jeopardy. We had to hope that she would come out alright in the end. The elements would overwhelm her if even one of the five representations of the elements moved. The other members were joined and if they broke the circle, hell would rain down on Savannah's vulnerability. To protect her, we needed to allow her ascension to finish, even if it meant watching her scream in anguish.

I couldn't watch Savannah any longer and instead looked at the other witches. Willow held a hand over her mouth, while tears streamed down her face. Maye's arms were crossed and I could see her fingernails digging into the skin of her arms. The expressions on each face contained worry, distress, and horror. Watching everyone else run through the emotions Savannah's pain evoked, was as bad as watching it myself.

I looked back at her. The strange substance coating her skin kept me from hearing her screams, but I could see them. She lay on the ground, while her body was taken by wave after wave of power; enough to shatter bones. The coating hardened and gained pigment. It terrified me that she was no longer visible. My only confirmation that she remained alive was her movements within the cocoon.

After the ascending hour had passed, we closed the circle and immediately rushed towards her. I knelt at her side to touch the object coating her skin. It felt like a bats wing; a hybrid of leather and wax.

"How do we get her out?" Willow knelt at my right and I looked up to see Maye and Josephine on the other side of Savannah.

"I don't know. Does anyone have a knife?" I looked around, but Josephine protested.

"You have no way of knowing how deep this goes. You might cut her. Besides, since we don't know what *this* is, we can't risk removing it. What if it's protecting her somehow?"

I ground my teeth. "What if it's hurting her somehow? Have you thought about that?"

"Here man." Griffin came to my shoulder and handed me his pocket knife. I flipped it open and touched the cocoon with it. Pressing gently, I tried to ease the knife in, but before I could slice my way through, the cocoon began to stretch. I could make out two hands pushing against the substance, try to claw their way through the layer.

"Move back!" Maye pushed everyone away from Savannah and we all watched as she emerged.

Somehow, I expected her to be coated in slime, but instead she her skin was decorated with a golden sheen. While that was stunning, I still wasn't prepared for the other changes. Savannah stood completely nude, but it was no longer the Savannah I knew. Her hair was long before, but now it hung to her thighs in wild curls. Maye placed a robe around Savannah's shoulders, but it had already seen that her body had matured. The silver in her eyes was almost blinding and her face had sharpened. Savannah had always looked young for her age, but now she looked exotic and womanly.

Maye ushered her back into the house, while the rest of us stood outside in shock. I sat on a boulder to wait for the other part of the ceremony, but I really wanted to take Savannah away and protect her. Everyone else stood around gossiping about the ascension, but Isis, Griffin, and Willow came to stand near me.

"What happened?" Isis proposed the question all of us were afraid to ask.

"I don't even like Savannah and that scared the hell out of me. You okay? You look like death." I looked up at Griffin's voice and tried to allay his fears with a forced smile.

"I'm fine. I don't know what that was, but I have never heard of something like that happening during an ascension." I looked over at Willow, who was staring at the house with wide eyes. "Willow, she'll be okay." I grabbed her hand to offer comfort and she looked down at me in grief.

"What if she's not f-ine? What if what happened to her has chang-ed her some-how?" Willow's voice broke several times, but I understood her fear.

A short while later Maye exited the house with Savannah at her side. Luckily, Savannah was clothed in a sundress that hid her body, but I knew it would be engraved on my mind for the rest of my life. The problem was that I knew it would stay with every guy in the coven too.

Savannah offered us a smile, as she entered the circle. Willow ran and threw her arms around Savannah; nearly knocking her over in the process. Savannah pulled Willow back, "I'm okay, really." She then wiped the tears from Willows cheeks and sat on the stool someone had placed in the center of the circle. The inscriptions had been washed from her skin, but it still glowed with an inner light.

Matthew, who was Josephine's husband, came to sit behind Savannah, while Josephine brought him a kit. He took the objects out and placed them on a cloth. The objects were to give a witch the symbol of her lineage on the day of her ascension. Today, Savannah would receive a permanent tattoo that only a member of the Cross family was allowed to wear. Matthew would use the ink that I had taken from the passageway. It was a mixture of blood from the founders of the Cross family and some other ingredients, which only a member of the Cross family was allowed to know.

Savannah didn't flinch when the boned needle pricked her flesh. She remained with her head slightly bent forward, and her hair tossed over her shoulder, while the symbol was tattooed onto the back of her neck. When Matthew was finished, Maye came forward to perform a healing spell to seal in the ink and prevent infection.

10 SUMMONING

Savannah

Willow wanted to perform the summoning a few days after my ascension, but I didn't feel up to it. Instead, I lazed around the house reading and practicing my magic. Now that I was more powerful, I needed to be more subtle when I tried to do something or I risked it spiraling out of control.

Liam came over every day to bring flowers, chocolates, and entertainment to keep me from boredom. While I appreciated Liam's efforts, whenever Ash saw him in the house, he went to Griffins. This meant I barely saw Ash, while I recovered from my ascension.

Willow and Izzy frequently dropped by after my ascension. Willow was filled with energy at solving my parents' mystery, but Izzy looked exhausted. I used deductive reasoning and figured Izzy was tired of Willow's enthusiasm. It wasn't exactly something to be excited over.

The night before the ritual would take place, I had a terrible dream. The demon was there. When he touched my skin, I could feel my essence flowing into him, while I became weaker and weaker. I was grateful when my cell phone woke me up. The clock said it was two in the morning, but I didn't care. Whoever was calling at this hour had saved me from a horrific nightmare.

"Hello." My voice was groggy, but I pushed to remain awake and sound coherent.

"Sa-van-nah…" The voice on the other end was pushing through tears. The sobs were loud and heavy.

"Izzy, what's wrong?"

"My mom died tonight." My entire world came crashing down in that moment.

"Are you at home?"

"Yeah…" The sobs continued. I climbed out of bed with the phone to my ear and threw on some clothes. I then walked through the bathroom to bang loudly on Ash's door.

The door clicked and Ash looked around it. "What is it?" He sounded concerned and then confused when he noticed the cell at my ear.

"I need you to drive me to Izzy's. Her mom passed away." He nodded and closed the door.

"Iz, I am coming over okay? Call Willow and stay on the line with her until I get there, okay?" Izzy was silent. "Promise me you will call Willow."

"Promise." The sobs had abated, but Izzy's voice sounded dead.

Ash was determined to get me to Izzy's as quickly as possible; he ran stop signs, the occasional light, and went 15 over the speed limit. He asked if I wanted him to come in with me, but I told him it was better if I went alone.

I thanked him and rushed to the door of the apartment building. I climbed the stairs and opened the door to Izzy's apartment. Once inside, I stopped in confusion. The apartment was unnaturally quiet. Izzy lay alone on the sofa, with the phone against her ear.

"Where is everyone?"

Izzy sat up with her arms tucked around her knees. "Take your pick; Dad's at the hospital filling out paperwork and Aunt Jen took the others back to her place. I didn't want to go anywhere until I got a chance to talk to you."

I nodded and sat beside her. She turned to sit with her back propped against the arm of the sofa. I could tell she had something important to say, but was reluctant.

"Izzy, it's okay. Just tell me what you want to say." She turned the phone off and placed it between us.

"I saw it."

"What did you see?" I looked in her eyes, while she searched for words.

"The demon was here." My eyes widened and before I could speak, Izzy motioned with her hand for me to remain silent. "I've been having these nightmares lately; about the demon. I thought it was because you and Willow were telling me about them. Tonight I got out of bed and saw a shadow moving in my mothers' room. My Dad was at work and my mother wasn't big enough to have a shadow that large. When I looked in the room, I saw it…" She broke into sobs.

I pulled Izzy into my arms and soothed her hair away from her face. "It's okay. I'm not going to let it hurt you."

"Savannah, it took something from her. This white smoke came out of her mouth and flowed into its mouth. I think Willow is right and the demon is feeding on people to gain power. It killed my mother and I bet it killed Jessica. Plus, a lot of other people in the surrounding towns have been dying mysteriously too."

Oh God. I couldn't stand to think that I was responsible for their deaths. I was the clumsy one, who tripped over the box. If I hadn't knocked the lid off, those people would still be alive. Izzy's mother would be alive. How was I ever going to fix this?

"Willow's coming over. She wants to do the summoning tonight. She's bringing the supplies."

Izzy sounded calm now. The summoning gave her a small portion of control in the face of this horrible event. I was not going to take that away from her, which is why I didn't protest performing the circle tonight. I thought it was a bad idea, but reasoned that the sooner we learned everything, the better we would be.

Willow arrived an hour later. We moved around the dining room furniture to create a clear space on the wooden floor. Izzy sat in one of the kitchen chairs, while Willow and I prepared the circle. Candles were placed to represent the five points of a pentacle. Symbols were etched into the wax of the candles to provide protection. Willow took a jar of dirt and poured it in a circle to connect the candles, but left an opening for Izzy to walk through.

Willow drew a pentacle within the circle, while I used an athame to slice open my palm. Witches rarely used blood in a ritual, but it was powerful and we needed protection from a demon. I allowed the blood to drip into a chalice, dipped a brush into the blood, and began drawing symbols within the star of the pentacle. We places object that represented the five elements at each point of the star to draw on for extra power. The outer circle would be for us, while the demon would be confined to the inner one.

"Izzy, were ready." Willow spoke in an absentminded voice, while she paged through her notebook.

Izzy took her place by the representation of air, while I closed off the outer circle. I then sat between spirit and water, which I would draw power from. Willow sat between earth and fire.

"Okay, what we need to do is clear our minds of outside influences. Your mind needs to be completely focused on the elements, my voice, and our task." Willow looked at Izzy as she spoke. I already knew the way to do a ritual, but Izzy was new at this.

I closed my eyes and concentrated on my breathing. When it was a steady rhythm, I sought my orb of power and encouraged it to spin. As it spun, I grasped threads and braided them together. I made three braids and sent one towards the spirit element and the other to the water element. The moment the braided strands collided with the elements, they lit up as bright as a star.

The end of the braids were attached to the elements, while the roots remained attached to my core. I grabbed the elemental braids, pulled to make them longer, and braided them with the third braid. I tied them into a lasso and I sent it out to wrap around the inner circle.

My braid of magic was like an electric blue current, while Willows was a soft green. Izzy's was barely noticeable against ours, but it was a pale orange. We exhibited some pressure and our braids expanded and spun to form a whirlpool. Willow began to speak the spell in Gaelic. Gaelic was a language of power, which was used for the most powerful spells. Her voice rose as the whirlpool gained speed and the apartment filled with a roaring sound.

A spark glimmered in the center, but it continuously shorted out before it could build enough power to remain stable. The spark resembled a lighter that had run out of lighter fluid, but created minor sparks when the metal was rolled. I willed more of myself into the braids and watched as the spark brightened to a constant glow. The eyes glowing within the whirlpool paralyzed me. *It* was watching us; it could see us. Panic set in, but I knew it was too late to turn back. Soon, the demon would step through the portal we had created. We were on a course that could not be broken; the point of no return.

A loud crack shook the apartment, making me think the demon was breaking through the circle. My chest tightened, while the crack changed to a shuttering, and suddenly a large portal appeared out of the wall behind Willow.

A terrifying sight stepped through the hole in the wall. It was a woman with flaming hair, flying behind her in an angry battle. Her eyes took in our circle, while she opened her mouth to let loose a high pitched howl. I had to cover my ears to prevent the sound from destroying my eardrums. The black hole behind her transformed into a vortex. Her howl heightened, while stretched her arm toward the whirlpool, and her hand slowly clenched. The whirlpool abated in sync with her hand until only a small portion remained. She gestured and the energized whirlpool was pulled into the vortex behind her.

"What in the nine hells are you three doing?"

With the whirlpool gone and the circle disbanded, I could make out what she was saying. I was grateful that she stopped howling, but it still took me a moment to process what she said. Willow had moved to stand with Izzy against the wall. They both stared in shock at the redhead.

"Who are you?" She looked familiar now that her hair had quieted and she was no longer shrieking.

"Who *I* am doesn't matter. What matters is why *you* thought it would be intelligent to summon a demon?" She crossed her arms, reminding me of Maye when she was angry.

I looked to Willow and Izzy for help, but they weren't helpful. I straightened, looked the redhead in the eye and prepared myself to speak. "Not that it's any of your business, but that demon was trapped in a box my parents hid. I accidentally unleashed it and now it is killing people. We didn't know what else to do. " I took a deep breath. "I answered your question, now answer mine." Crossing my arms, I attempted to look intimidating.

She sighed. "My name is Kali and I just stopped you from getting yourselves *killed*. *Demons* do not like to be summoned, but what you were summoning was far worse than the average demon." She walked over, grabbed a chair, and straddled the back of the chair.

"Wh-what was it then?" Izzy spoke, but her question came out as a squeak.

"Do any of you know the story of the fallen angels?" Silence greeted her question, while we exchanged glances. Kali rested her arms on the back of the chair and propped her chin on them. "The angels who fell from heaven became the rulers of demons. Most of the fallen became generals of the demonic armies, but the original fallen became the rulers of the nine circles of hell. Are you following?"

"I think so. So, the fallen angels became like princes?" I shuddered at the thought.

"Yes. There were many different types of angels within heaven. Above all others, the archangels were the most powerful and dangerous. think of them as heaven's soldiers. Archangels, being the most loyal to heaven remained at their post. However, a single archangel fell. His name was Asmodeus, but he is known by many names. Asmodeus was given the rank of arch demon is the highest ranking prince of hell. He was the one you were summoning."

"What? You have got to be kidding me!" I felt sick, but forced myself to hold it together for Willow and Izzy.

"Your parents entrapped him when you were just a babe. Do not try to summon him again." Kali stood.

"Wait! How do I fix this? How do I stop him from hurting everyone?" I was desperate. I ran and grabbed her arm. She turned back to look at my hand gripping her and looked into my eyes. At first, she seemed angry, but the anger seeped away and kindness took its place.

"I know you feel responsible." Kali sighed, and looked away. "I would guess that you need to figure out what your parents did to him, other than trapping him. Figure out why he is sticking around, when he could leave and gain power elsewhere. Oh, and try not to deliberately piss him off; unless you have a death wish." She snorted and left through the door.

Izzy, Willow, and I barely discussed Kali and Asmodeus during the following days. We were more concerned with the death of Izzy's mother, but the demon haunted our every move. The community experienced more deaths and they weighed on us.

11 DEALS IN SEDUCTION

Liam

Against my mothers' wishes, I gave Savannah her space the week after Izzy's mother died. It seemed wrong to try to seduce her, while her best friend was grieving. After a week, I decided it was time to cheer her up.

My mother hosted a small gathering of the leading members from the coven. I brought Savannah as my date, but my mother stole her from my arm, and introduced her to the everyone. It irritated me to see my mother show Savannah off, as though she were a prized jewel she recently purchased. I stopped watching them after a while. I knew that my mother considered me bringing Savannah here, as my duty. Though, I would rather be anywhere else right now.

"Liam, if you continue to wear that sour expression, Savannah may begin to believe you're not enjoying her company." My mothers' voice startled me. I had been so lost in my thoughts that I didn't hear her approach.

"How could she think that? You have kept her from my company the entire night." I sipped my whiskey, grateful for the numbness that spread throughout my body. It made my mother's company less hampering.

"Perhaps, if you were more social you would have remained with her. You can't avoid your responsibilities forever. It's time to be welcomed back into the fold. Tonight, would be the perfect time to start."

"Mother, you can be so charming sometimes." My voice was laced with sarcasm. "Did you forget why I left?" I glanced at her through my peripheral vision. "Just be glad I brought *her* and leave *me* be. I could always complain of a headache. Savannah would leave with me then."

"You wouldn't do that, because you know that if you did, I would make your life a living hell." She sighed and shook her head. "Make certain you don't forget why you are spending time with her to begin with."

"I could never forget. You remind me every chance you get. Besides, there is no way Savannah will choose our coven over her family. She loves them too much."

"If you gave her an ultimatum she might."

She didn't leave me room to respond and walked quickly towards the group surrounding Savannah. I wanted to shout obscenities at her back and maybe use a glass to knock some sense in her. Women did not like ultimatums and I would never ask Savannah to choose between me and her family. It's wrong. That's why I hadn't tried to take our relationship to the next level. The truth was that I didn't want her to end up in a coven where she would be unhappy.

Savannah looked at me through the mob of people surrounding her. It was a pleading gaze, telling me she was overwhelmed. I grinned and shook my head to signal she was on her own. She made a pained expression and I decided to take pity on her.

"Excuse me. I need some time alone with Savannah. I promised her we would take a walk in the gardens." Reluctantly, the crowd parted and Savannah dashed through.

"Thank you. I couldn't breathe." She spoke in a whisper, as we walked through the terrace doors and down the stairs. "Are they always like that?"

"Just for you, princess."

"I'm the lucky guinea pig, huh? I feel so special." She gazed around at the extensive gardens. "It's beautiful here."

I looked over at her, while she walked ahead to trail her fingers against the petals. In the moonlight, her hair was the color of the night. Soft blue highlights gathered in her curls where the light touched them.

"After our walk in the gardens, we will meet everyone in the barn for the circle." I was hesitant to mention the circle, because Savannah hadn't been thrilled about the idea during the ride over here.

"I'm kind of nervous Liam. I know you said Diamante wants it to be a surprise, but I don't like it. You can't expect me to overcome the stereotypes about dark covens this quickly. Can you please just tell me what we will be doing?"

I smiled. "I don't think so. It's more fun to keep you in the dark. I promise it won't be anything bad, the coven just wants to give you a gift; something special."

"But does it have to be a surprise?" Savannah made a puppy dog face, but I only laughed. "You'll just have to wait and see."

"Fine," Savannah muttered as she looked around.

We walked through the sprawling gardens, along a path lined with tulips and carnations. The terrace beside the garden was covered in roses that climbed the walls.

A barn emerged from the twilight, as we rounded a path. "Is that where we are going to meet everyone?" Savannah asked, as she looked up at the rustic red barn.

"Yep, everyone should already be inside." We walked up to the door and Savannah reached for its handle.

"Before we go in, you have to promise me you won't get scared." I thought about my mother's plans and knew it would be easy for Savannah to make the wrong assumptions.

Savannah's eyes narrowed in suspicion. "Why, is there something in there I should be afraid of? If this is something that can hurt me I don't want to do it."

"No, it's nothing like that, but if you have never seen this kind of magic before it can be a bit startling." I hurriedly grabbed her hands to soothe her.

"And you're sure nothing in there will hurt me?" She narrowed her eyes.

"I would never do anything to hurt you." I kissed her, and she looked into my eyes with a dazed expression.

"Promise?"

"I promise," I said, while chuckling.

"Alright then." Savannah said, as she reached out and pulled the doors open.

Savannah

The barn was well lit with rows of candles set in braces. Members of the Sacred Moon coven were standing around talking. A few farm implements had been moved to the side of the barn, away from the main group of people, and near the hay. The floor had been swept to clear the piles of hay.

In the center of the floor was a large crimson circle. I ignored everything else, when I saw what was lying in the center of the circle. It was the largest black feline I had ever seen. It was a black panther.

I started to back away from the large cat, but Liam put his arm around my shoulders and whispered, "Don't worry, it won't hurt you. We're keeping it calm."

"You said that nothing in here would hurt me! Why is there a freaking panther in the middle of the floor?" I demanded angrily. Several scenarios were spinning through my mind, but the worst was that they might want to sacrifice the animal.

"He's part a gift to you from the coven. We wanted to surprise you. Before you even ask, we're not going to hurt him."

"Then why is he here and what exactly am I supposed to do with a panther? Maye would flip if I brought it home and that's assuming it doesn't rip my throat out first!" My fingers lifted to my throat. I had never considered it before, but I would really like to keep my neck intact.

"My mother will explain."

"Ah." called a voice from the group, "There you two are. I was beginning to worry."

Liam's mother, Diamante strode forward in one of the most beautiful dresses I had ever seen. A flowing emerald colored gown, which fell off the shoulders in layers of a darker green. The dress was embellished with emerald stones around the waist and neckline.

"We have been waiting for you." Diamante said, as she stepped towards Liam and gestured to me.

"Why is there a panther in the middle of the floor?" I forced the question before I lost my nerve.

Diamante smiled. "He is a gift for you. He will help to show you the world, as you have never known it. There is no need to be frightened. He will not harm you, and he knows that he is with friends"

"Who…what are we going to do?" I stammered.

"We are going to bond you with a spirit animal my dear," replied Diamante. "Come, we must begin soon."

"What does that mean?" I turned to Liam and asked, as Diamante led me to the circle.

Diamante replied softly, as she moved me into the circle. "This beautiful creature will be with you always, as your friend and protector. Once you have bonded, you will be able to take his form."

A warm tingle of excitement ran down my back, as I knelt down besides the panther's head, but ice quickly followed. "What happens when he dies? Will I die too?"

Diamante shook her head. "No, you don't understand. He is already close to death. This is called a bond for a reason. His spirit will become a part of you, and his soul will live on inside you."

Diamante held out her right hand, palm up and white smoke wisped from her finger tips. The smoke twisted together, tore apart into strands of smoke, which extended to transform into wings. Finer wisps merged into the shape of a head and beak.

In a matter of seconds, a falcon make of smoke appeared above Diamante's hand. The falcon's eyes were deep green to match the stones on her dress. "This is Celeste." The falcon opened its beak, and although there was no sound, the air vibrated with its call. Diamante closed her hand and the falcon faded into mist.

I reached out to brush my fingers down the back of the panther's head and he shifted to lay his head in my lap. I smiled as I stroked his fur, and a deep rumbling grew in his chest.

Diamante spoke at my ear. "Excellent, he likes you."

"Will this hurt him?" I asked with worry building inside me.

"No, you will be easing him from pain. He lived a hard life before he came into our care."

"What happened to him?" I asked and looked up.

"You will see." Diamante said softly, as she motioned for the rest of the coven to take their places around the circle. "Remain calm Savannah. I promise you this will not hurt, but it will be like nothing you have ever experienced before."

I looked down into the big cats eyes, and murmured, "What's his name?"

"Kit," replied Diamante before beginning a slow chant. One by one, the rest of the group matched her rhythm.

I remained looking down into the panther's dark eyes. They grew larger, until his eyes filled my field of vision and my world went black. Seconds creped by and a speck of light appeared. It expanded until it was all I knew.

I reached out to touch the colors within the light. Suddenly, I was being taken from my mother to be placed in a box. When I tried to jump free and run back to my mother, something grabbed my neck and pushed me towards the darkness.

I jerked my hand back from the colors. What I had just felt, were Kit's memories and he had been terrified. I knew what it was like to be young and afraid, but Kit's yearning for his mother was unfamiliar to me. I sank my fingers into the colorful array once more.

I was trapped in a cage, while each day new people came to stare at me. When all the people had gone, the man with the stick would hit me, before throwing a few meager scraps of meat into my cage. I was hungry and tired.

A tear trickled down my cheek at what this poor animal had endured. I knew what it was like to be caged and tortured each day. I could relate to feeling lost and alone, while being surrounded by a darkness that threatened to consume me

I was in Kit's cage and could barely move. I had no energy and my body ached. A tall woman handed the man with the stick a thick envelope and walked over to the cage. She knelt down and looked me in the eyes. I saw the woman's compassion before she spoke.

"You are safe now, little one. My name is Diamante, and you will be part of my family now. No one will ever hurt you again." My chest rumbled, but for the first time in my life it was not because of fear or anger. It was hope.

My hand dropped to my side and tears fell freely down my cheeks. The light faded, and distant chanting grew louder. The darkness faded into color and I was again within the circle. Kit's body was gone, but his memories were imprinted on my soul.

Liam

I opened the door and Savannah walked through before me. "Do you want something to drink?"

"Um, do you have any soda?" I nodded and headed to the kitchen to grab a sprite. When I came back into the living room, I found Savannah fidgeting.

"Afraid I might bite? Please tell me you don't think I'm some kind of monster that is going to pounce on you?" Her silence confirmed her worry. "Princess, I have never needed to pounce on any female. They usually pounce on me."

"What females?" She gave me a sour look and I had to laugh, which seemed to anger her.

"Princess, how could you believe that there are any other females in my life right now? It's just you." I deposited a chaste kiss on her lips.

I meant to restrain myself from anything other than friendliness, until I knew for sure that she wasn't still hurting over Izzy's mother's death. However, having gone an entire week without her, I couldn't help myself. I pulled her into my arms and ravaged her mouth. I rained kisses along her neck and back to her lips, but when I moved my hand to caress her breast, she stiffened.

"I'm sorry. I should have asked." I wasn't in the habit of asking, but Savannah wasn't a promiscuous woman. Kali was right, when she said that Savannah was not the type of woman I was used to.

"It's not that. It's..." She paused. "I've never done anything more than kiss a guy. I don't know what I am supposed to do." Her brows furrowed and she looked embarrassed. "I want to, but I just don't know *how*."

Grabbing her face, I looked her directly in the eyes. "You don't have to learn *how* right now. We can take it slow. I don't want us to do anything you aren't ready for." I kissed her forehead and smoothed back her hair. "I'll be right back." I walked into my bedroom, closed the door, and attempted to pull myself together. I wasn't used to reining myself in, but until I gained my composure I needed to take a breather.

Savannah

I watched Liam retreat into his room. I couldn't believe how understanding he was being. It was a relief, because as much as I wanted him, I wanted to figure a few things out before our relationship progressed.

I walked over to the coffee table and picked up the soda, Liam had left there. As I took a sip, his phone beeped, and his mothers' name lit the screen. Worried that it might be important, I lifted the cell phone from the table to see what the text said. My soda dropped from my hands, while I reeled from the content of the extremely detailed text.

I hope you plan to take my advice from earlier. She has already gone through her ascension. It won't be long before the coven will want her to take her initiation vows. If we have any hope of luring her into our coven, you need to seduce her now. You can't keep putting it off. I know that you didn't want this assignment, but the Cross girl is powerful and an alliance with her will be mutually beneficial. Seduce her and give her the ultimatum. Once she has joined our coven, you can go back to sleeping with as many humans as you would like.

I was shocked. Liam had been pretending this entire time? I was an *assignment?* I tossed his cell phone on the table and looked back at the door to his bedroom. I felt torn. One piece of my soul insisted on confronting him, while the other desperately wished to flee. I felt raw and betrayed. How could I have thought I meant something to him? Why had I been so stupid? I left the apartment and ran down the street before opening my cell to text Izzy.

Izzy picked me up a short while later to take me home. I knew she could see how upset I was, but for once she didn't push me to talk. She let the silence soothe me and I was grateful for it.

Izzy stopped in front of my house, and said, "Savannah, if you need anything or just want to talk... call me, okay?" I nodded and bolted from the car. My feet couldn't move fast enough to propel me towards the house. I was fleeing a tsunami that threatened to wash away the safety net I built around my core.

I ran into the house with tears streaming down my face. I came to a quick stop in the hall, when Ash bared my path. Backing up, I tried to avoid him, but he wouldn't allow it. His arm snatched out to grab me around my waist and lifted me into his arms, to cradle me.

"What's wrong?"

I struggled in his arms, kicking my legs and wiggling to get free. When that failed, I started pounding on his chest with my fists. "Let me down!"

Ash laughed. "Well, this seems familiar!"

"What is that supposed to mean?" I crossed my arms and pouted, while giving him a cold stare.

"The first day we met I carried you into the house and you struggled just like this. Remember?"

I became more pliant and my tears stopped. "Put me down, Ash."

His face became serious as he lowered me gently to the ground. He kept his arm wrapped around my waist and my body pressed to his. His body protected me from the rogue wave that massaged my emotions in a turmoil. The safety net Liam endangered was now more solid than ever before. Ash held it together, he pressed the rope, and maneuvered it to a placement that allowed me to breathe once more.

"I'm not letting you go until I know what's wrong. Did Liam do something to you?" My face froze. Ash's arm dropped and he growled. The house shuddered as the noise echoed against the walls. "I'm going to kill him!"

Ash pushed past me. I rushed to stop him, but he spun around to push me away. Throwing my arms around his neck, I massaged his lips with mine. At first his body was still, but then he relaxed and pulled me closer. He was like a starved man, using my mouth to sate his hunger. It was an passionate kiss fueled by his anger. My blood simmered at the contact, forcing my body to be instinctively wanton. Ash tried to slow the kissing, but I pressed harder and gyrated against his hips in a sensual dance. He groaned and backed me up until my heels hit the staircase.

Ash didn't falter at the inconvenience the stars proposed. He lifted my legs to straddle his waist, climbed the stairs, while kissing me with renewed passion. I couldn't think, breath or deny the electric charge between us. Suddenly, every aspect of myself was desperate to have him; all of him.

Ash kicked his bedroom door open, slammed the door behind us and pushed my back against it. His hands slipped up my thighs to gently push my dress up a few inches. This evoked a purr from deep within my chest.

Against my lips, Ash spoke. "Did you just purr?" I laughed, and pressed my breasts against his chest. I held onto him, chaining him to the fervor, forcing him to succumb. The rhythm of my heart beat faster to match his. I didn't want anything between us; I just wanted him.

Tearing at Ash's shirt, the buttons scattered across the floor. His shirt soon followed. His lips moved away from mine, but before I could protest the lost contact, he rained kissed down my neck to my shoulder. He slipped the strap down and held it to reveal my milky skin.

I felt overwhelmed and pulled him back to my lips. My hands skimmed across his chest to lay flat against his firm abdomen. He groaned, while I nibbled on his lower lip. My hands lowered to unbutton his jeans, but he pulled away. I grabbed his neck to pull him back, but he took my hands to pry them away with a determined intensity. "Maye will be home any minute." He took my left hand and kissed the palm before putting more space between us.

I stood still, trying to understand what had just happened, and failing to dispel the energy surging through me. Ash's face was flushed and his chest gleaned from our efforts. I had an urge to lick the moisture that trailed down the planes of his stomach.

"What did Liam do?" I shook my head to beat out the sexual thoughts and focused entirely on his words.

"Ugh, I don't want to talk about it." I walked to the adjoining bathroom, but he pulled me back against his chest.

Whispering in my ear, he said "If you don't tell me what he did, I am going to assume the worst and hunt him down. The way I promised him I would if he hurt you."

"Fine!" I jerked my body away from Ash. "He was dating me, because his mother ordered him to. They wanted me to join their coven." My voice caught on the last word. Ash spun me to face him, with a concerned expression on his face.

"It's their loss. You wouldn't really have left us, would you?"

"Of course I wouldn't. I just feel so stupid." I covered my face with my palms, as though hiding my embarrassment, but I knew it was futile.

Ash leaned forward to gently kiss the tip of my nose. "Don't. They're the stupid ones. Besides, it's going to be nice not seeing Liam anywhere near you." His right side of his mouth quirked up in satisfaction.

I smacked his shoulder and danced into my bedroom. I didn't hurt anymore. Ash had healed the crater Liam had left in my heart. It merely took a frenzied make out session to erase the emotional decay that had eaten at me earlier.

I was beginning to feel fickle, but the truth is that even when I was with Liam, I had wanted Ash. Now that Liam was out of the picture, I ached marginally, but Ash bared me from any further pain.

It wasn't long before Maye came home to find me lying on my bed. I remained on my back with my gaze fixated on the ceiling. At least, that is what it would look like to everyone else. I was actually sorting through Kit's memories. It was interesting to look at the world through the eyes of a cat. They processed their memories differently and relied heavily on senses rather than emotions. Emotions were developed over time, but once they had grown, they remained firmly in place. A feline could love with an intensity that humans couldn't match.

"Darling, how was your date with Liam?"

I turned onto my side and propped my head up with my hand. "Let's just put it this way, you were right… he's bad news. I should have taken Josephine's vision more seriously." I allowed my head to plop back onto my pillow with a vengeance.

"I take it that means you won't be seeing him anymore?" Her voice sounded annoyingly optimistic.

"You guessed right. Please, just don't ask for more details."

"Alright, child. If you decide you need to talk, you know where to find me." Instead of leaving my room, as I expected, Maye came forward to sit on my bed. "Is there something going on between you and Ash?"

I sat up straight and scooted as far from her as possible. I racked my brain for the right thing to say, but the truth was that I didn't really know what was going on between me and Ash. We hadn't defined the changed between us or what it meant for the future. How could I answer Maye's question, when even I didn't know the answer?

"I don't know." I said, decisively.

"You don't know or you don't want to say?" I remained silent, because it was a little of both. "Child, I love you and Ash. I've watched your relationship grow. If you have feelings for one another don't worry about my acceptance. I want the best for both of you. Now, give me a kiss. I'm going to bed." I kissed her cheek and she laughed, as she exited the room.

"Well, that's a relief." I was shocked, when Ash pushed the door open.

"You were eavesdropping?" My pillow hit him square in the chest.

"The door was open and sound carries in this house. You expect me to ignore your conversation when I am the subject of it?"

"Yes, no, I don't know! It's just rude! What if we were having a private conversation?" Ash could be so frustrating sometimes, but he was also strangely adorable.

"Well, if that were the case, I would recommend closing the door and talking in a whisper. Otherwise, it's impossible for it to be *private*." He laughed and moved forward. "So, what *is* going on between us?"

I couldn't look him in the eyes. I felt bare in front of him. My other pillow lay on the bed in front of me; I grabbed the pillow and wrapped my arms around it. "What do you think is going on between us? Other than all the kissing…"

Ash sighed, "I think you like kissing me and I think that you shouldn't be kissing anyone else." His eyebrow raised to question how I felt about it.

"I do. Like kissing you, that is… Now that I know the truth about Liam, I don't plan to be kissing anyone else anytime soon." I shrugged and avoided his eyes. Instead, I focused on my quilt.

"*Ever*. You don't plan to kiss anyone *ever* again."

The dangerous possessiveness I had seen at the bonfire was back. Ash's intimidated me when his back straightened and his pupils melted to an acidic fire. I half wanted to flee the intensity that filled the room, but the other part of me…yearned for him? The feeling began in my throat, trailed along the side of my neck, and rushed down my spine to pool in the lower half of my body.

This was something new. Evidently, I am the type of woman who likes a possessive alpha male …Huh, who would have thought?

"Ash, I can't promise that and I am not going to lie to make you feel better. I can promise that you are the only guy I want to be kissing, now." I nibbled on my lip in uncertainty, because I knew this conversation was going to change the fabric of our relationship. It was as though we had spent years sewing a quilt and now we were removing the stitching to start over.

"S, we can't do this half way. You know that, right? I mean, you are either mine or you're not. Half and half won't work, because it would ruin our relationship."

I nodded. I had been worrying over the same thing. We stood balanced on a teeter totter. Once small move on either part could leave one or both of us sprawled against the sandy ground. "Let me sleep on it. I'll give you my answer first thing tomorrow. Okay?"

Ash nodded. "That's reasonable, but S?" I looked up. "Make sure that you are certain about your decision, okay?" He didn't wait for my response, but closed the bathroom door firmly behind him.

I watched the door for what seemed like forever. I was afraid of what it would mean to make the decision, because it would impact our relationship forever. I wasn't even certain I should be making a decision like this given everything that was going on. I just got out of my first relationship and still felt betrayed. Plus, the demon was still out there and I hadn't figured out what to do about that.

Something moved within me and Kit appeared in spirit form to pace around my room. His fur was silvery blue and his lengthy form took up most of my room. He sniffed the perfume on my dresser and sneezed; shaking his head in agitation. I laughed, when he pawed at the bottle, pushing it away from him. His eyes were curious as he paraded around to examine every corner of my bedroom. Once he was satisfied, he fell to the floor on his back, and wiggled his body in contentment. He kept his eyes on mine, while rubbing his back against the floor.

It was amusing to watch a panther cavorting like a kitten, but I needed to get some rest. I changed into a white satin slip, climbed under the covers and patted the blanket. Kit jumped onto the bed to lay his head on my legs with the rest of his body squeezed against my side. I thought he would be heavy, but the pressure was no more than the weight of a feather.

I remained awake, thinking about everything that had happened to me in such a short time. I wasn't sure what I wanted to do about Ash, but I didn't think I could avoid kissing him. I couldn't kiss him and keep our relationship as it had always been. Ash explicitly stated that it was all or nothing. I would have to choose *all*, because I couldn't face being left with *nothing*.

My decision was made. Sensing my peace, Kit raised himself over me and his spirit sank back into my flesh. We became one again and I was reassured by his presence. At least there was one amazing gift Liam had left me. I would cherish Kit for the rest of my life, however long that would be.

12 DIVINE ENERGY

In sync with my recent dreams, the demon plagued my every vision. I worried that he might be really affecting my dreams. I reasoned that if he could haunt me in person, why would he choose to terrorize my dreams? Wouldn't reality be worse than fantasy?

Asmodeus's face swam into my vision and I struggled to get away. His arms grasped me to squeeze the air from my lungs. I tried to pull away from the darkness, but it smothered me, pulled me down into its oceanic depths. I began to hyperventilate, while crying for someone to help me. Did my thoughts lure him to my dreams? Had he come to finish what he started?

I forced myself to be still and breathe evenly. Blackness permeated my eyesight, but my other senses sharpened. I squirmed in an attempt to escape my assailant until I breathed in the smell of wildflowers. A cool breeze tossed my hair into my mouth, and I heard leaves flutter. I was in the forest. *This* was my territory. I knew this forest and I could easily find my way home once a chance to escape presented itself. Willow and I had built a fort here when we were younger. I usually sought it when I was troubled and thought it would make a wonderful hide out.

My attacker stopped to set me against a tree trunk. The wood rubbed my shoulder blades raw through the satin fabric of my nightgown. I felt vulnerable. A rush of air collided with my frame, but before I could kick my abductor; he took off my blindfold.

My eyes swam with tears, but focused enough to see Ash smiling at me. I slapped him. "What the hell are you doing? Are you crazy?" I smacked him, as he laughingly danced out of reach.

"You said you would give me an answer *first thing tomorrow*. It's midnight, which is first thing tomorrow." He held his hands in front of him, as if expecting me to launch an attack.

"Ash! I meant after a night's rest! How could you do that to me? I thought you were someone trying to kill me!"

Ash cleared his throat and looked around, causing me to take in my surroundings. My jaw dropped. We were standing in a place of divine energy. Places of divine energy were inordinately powerful and hidden from ordinary humans. Witches had to cross a threshold of power to access them. There were only certain times, when we could cross the threshold. Witchlings weren't allowed to enter these places, but I wasn't a witchling any longer.

Divine places had been described to me many times, but never had their description lived up to the reality. I was standing in a field surrounded by a forest. A full moon brightened the star in the sky. Colored lights, which resembled the aurora borealis glistened across the inky blanket. The moon highlighted the azure flowers that pollinated the field. Everything had an dream-like inner glow. Animals weren't afraid of us here; a deer grazed in the far parts of the field near the foliage of the forest, while a falcon watched from a nearby branch.

"It's beautiful." I walked into the field of flowers and trailed my fingers against them. Tingling started in my fingers and quickly spread to the rest of my body. The sensation intoxicated me. Laughing, I spun in a circle with my arms stretched wide.

Ash stood a few feet away and watched my excitement with an amused smirk. "There is a reason why they call this a divine place." He nodded towards the flowers. "Taste the petals." I looked at him in disgust.

"Ew… I don't make a habit of eating flowers. I'm more of a meat and potatoes kind of girl."

"Nothing in this place is as it seems. Seriously, try it." He picked a flower and handed it to me.

I looked around and realized that he was probably right. This placed looked, felt, sounded, and even smelled different. Why wouldn't it taste different? Shrugging, I plucked a petal and hesitantly placed it onto my tongue. It didn't taste the way I expected. Instead, the taste was like pure emotion centered on my tongue. The petal liquefied as I rubbed it between my tongue and the roof of my mouth. The petal went straight to my head and intensified my emotions.

"Oh my God, this is amazing!" I looked at the flower in shock and back at Ash. "Is everything like this? I mean, do the leaves taste like this too or is it only the flowers?"

"Everything tastes different, but I don't recommend eating bark; it's a little too tough and I don't think you would enjoy having splinters in your tongue."

Kit could feel my joy and emerged from my body to run across the field. The deer looked up at the intrusion and hurriedly went back to eating.

"What the hell is that?" Ash jumped back several feet and looked at Kit in horror.

"That is Kit. He's the only good thing I got out of my relationship with Liam." Kit rushed back and butted his head against Ash's hip, which nearly knocked him over.

"Okay. How did you get *Kit*?" He still had a stricken face, but he had warmed to Kit and was petting the panther.

"He was dying and Liam's coven performed a bonding ceremony. Kit is my spirit animal; I can take his shape and he can live in transparent form outside of my body." Ash nodded in acceptance and pulled me into his arms.

"You owe me an answer."

Seizing the change of subject, I danced out of his reach and attempting to be coy. "Hmmm… I think this place is a little too distracting. I don't know if I will be able to give you an answer." I looked around, laughed, and ran for the forest. I jumped over logs, ducked beneath branches, and moved as far into the forest as my feet could take me. Ash made noise as he ran to catch up to me and quickened my steps.

I halted when I came to a lake. It was different from the sort of lakes I knew of. The water resembled liquefied silver, but it was thin enough to swim in. I knelt at the edge of the water, trailed my fingers through it, and watched as it came alive. The liquid substance traveled up my arm and onto my shoulder. I started to panic, but the water transformed into a small bird and rubbed its head against my cheek.

"Scared?" Ash spoke at my shoulder and scratched the liquid bird between its wings.

"Does the water always do this? Does it normally take the shape of animals?"

"No, not really. It probably sensed your curiosity and was attempting to soothe you."

"Wait, the water is an empath? What happens if you swim in it?"

Ash sighed. "Yes, the water here is a living being and an empath." Laughing, he continued. "I don't think the water would mind if you take a swim. Though, you should know that the water affects inhibitions."

"Hmmm... what type of *inhibitions*?" I pushed the strap of my dress off my shoulder and the other soon followed. "Don't watch!"

"I think it's a little late to tell you what kind of inhibitions." He said, as he turned away from me.

I pushed my nightgown past my breasts and over my hips to let it fall around my feet. I wasn't wearing a bra, but I kept my silk underwear on. The water was warm around my hips. It moved up to cover the length of my skin below my neck. I floated on my back before letting my feet to sink toward the bottom.

"Ash, are you going to leave me to enjoy this on my own? Come on, get in here!"

He turned back to face me. "Give me an answer and I will. Otherwise, you can meet me back by the threshold."

I thought about making him beg, but thought better of it when he started walking away. "Yes! My answer is yes!"

"Yes, meaning *all*?" I nodded in confirmation and he quickly stripped down to his boxers.

My heart beat raced, when he swam close to me. He dipped his head beneath the water and shook the excess liquid from it. Smoothing his hair away from his face, I slid my hand down to his shoulder, biceps, chest, and finally his abs. He pulled me close, until my naked breasts pressed against his chest and sucked in his breath sharply.

"Maybe this wasn't such a good idea." Grabbing his head, I pulled it down to kiss me. I enjoyed his reaction to me. It made me feel a combination of excitement and power.

Ash set me away from him and splashed some water in my direction. "I think someone needs to cool off."

"Mmmm…and you don't?" He laughed, but we both knew he didn't need to answer the question.

We swam for a while; playfully dunking each other and splashing. When I walked out of the water, I expected to have to wait a while to dry off, but the water trailed off my form, leaving my skin pleasantly dry.

Ash led us back to the field of flowers and to the threshold. While witches could only enter a divine place at certain times, we could leave whenever we wanted. Before we stepped over the threshold, Ash stopped me. He kissed me deeply once more. Then we held hands and walked through the threshold.

Ash

Last night had been more amazing than I had hoped. The joy on Savannah's face, in response to the purity of the divine place, was the happiest I had ever seen her. I walked into the halls of my high school with a wicked grin on my face, which is how Griffin and Isis found me.

"What's with you?" Isis wasn't used to me smiling anywhere near her.

"Wouldn't you like to know?" I stopped when I saw their faces. They looked grim.

"She means, why are you so happy after what happened?" Griffin grabbed my shoulder. "I thought you would have more sense than that."

"Whoa." I held my hands up in defeat. "What happened?"

Griffin and Isis looked at one another and Griffin nodded. "Another kid died last night a few towns over. You didn't hear?" I nodded. "Remember Michael?"

"Michael, the shy guy on the baseball team?" I tried to grasp an image of him, but had trouble remembering conjuring an image of him. Isis nodded.

Griffin swiped his fingers through his hair and looked around to make sure no one was watching us. "That's not all. Michael went on a lunatic rage last night and killed his whole family. Then today, a kid dropped dead in the hall and two others had psychotic breaks. They were removed to a mental health ward."

"All that happened this morning? First period hasn't even started yet!" I couldn't believe what was happening around here, but I was beginning to worry that something supernatural was happening. These occurrences couldn't be coincidences.

"That's why school was called off for the rest of the week." I turned at Savannah's voice and saw Willow and Izzy standing with her.

"Hey, Savannah. How are you feeling? I haven't seen you since your ascension." We all looked at Isis in shock. "What? I can't be worried? She looked like she was being bathed in the flames of hell! Even I was worried." She shrugged, as if being worried about others was a common occurrence for her.

"Um, I'm okay. I guess…" Savannah crinkled her eyes and shifted from one foot to the other.

"That's great! If you need anything…" Seeing our faces, Isis made an irritated sound and stomped off. Griffin soon followed.

I turned back to Savannah. "That was weird. What are your plans today? I mean, since we don't have school." I wasn't sure if Izzy and Willow knew about last night, but I wanted to spend the day with Savannah. I could already feel my lips against hers, while she pressed her body to mine.

"She is hanging with us today. She already promised." Izzy's voice was laced with venom, unlike her normal cheerful self. Willow didn't look much happier.

"Alright. Alright! She's all yours." I grabbed Savannah's hand and held her eyes, as I slowly kissed her palm; savoring the contact. "I will see you later." She nodded and I walked away to gain my composure.

I located Griffin and Isis in the parking lot. The three of us decided to see a movie and get some lunch. It was early afternoon when I arrived at home.

"Maye! You home?" I called out, with no answer. Instead, I heard voices murmuring in the living room. Following the sound, I found Savannah and Liam in a deep discussion.

"What the hell is *he* doing here?" I rushed forward to pull Liam off the couch, but Maye came out of nowhere and dragged me into the hallway.

"Think with your head, boy. What is throwing him out going to do other than anger Savannah?"

I stopped trying to press my way into the room and looked at Maye helplessly. "What should I do, then? After what he did to Savannah, I'm supposed to just leave him alone?" I spoke through ground teeth.

"Yes. Savannah is a big girl and she can handle herself. Leave them be."

Maye walked away with a look of pity. I sat on the stairs with my head in my lap. I could hear Savannah and Liam talking, but I couldn't make out what they were saying. I comforted myself with the thought that if they were talking, they weren't kissing.

Liam walked into the hallway and stood at the door to wait for Savannah. A few minutes later, she walked up to him with an apology for making him wait. Her back was to me when she leaned up to hug Liam. He buried his face in her hair, squeezed tight and gave her a lingering kiss on the lips. My insides screamed at their kiss, but I forced myself to remain still. I turned my gaze to a used a picture that hung on the wall next to the door. I used the painting as a focal point and bit my lip. My lungs started to burn, but I refused to allow them control.

I was concentrating on the willow tree in the picture, when it began to smoke and caught fire. The flames released my tension, which made me slow to react. When Savannah started shouting, I stood quickly. The flames were traveling up the photo to lick the wall. She looked at me in horror, while I tore off my shirt and hit the frame to knock it from the wall. I used my shirt to smother the painting until only smoke remained. Meanwhile, Liam rushed towards the kitchen to get the fire extinguisher.

Liam came back into the room and stopped. I followed the line of his sight to see Savannah standing with her arm stretched towards the wall. The fire that had traveled up the wall was now frozen. We turned in unison when Maye stumbled into the hallway. Her hands were covered in dirt and she held a spade in one hand. Her expression was as icy, as the flames Savannah froze.

"My, what happened here? Are you all okay?" Maye looked us over for injuries and then at the ice laced wall.

"Oh dear, that wall is charred to pieces." She sighed, seeing my guilt ridden face. "Hmmm...I suppose you are responsible for this?"

I cleared my throat and glanced back and forth at Savannah and Maye. "Yes, but it was an accident."

"I'm sure it was. I remember your father had a similar *accident*, when your parents had a nasty fight. You need to control your emotions, Ash. I don't think that the insurance company will be too happy with me if you burn this house down." She shook her head and waved her hands at the three of us to get out of the house. We left the door open to allow the house to breathe and moved away.

"Sorry about that." Savannah apologized to Liam and walked him to his car. I stood and watched. This time there was no kiss.

"Ash..."

I held up my hand to ward of her questions. "Why were you kissing him?"

"That? It was a goodbye kiss! It was a harmless peck."

I bared my teeth at her. "*That* was *not* a goodbye kiss. A goodbye kiss is a peck on the cheek or a chaste one on the lips! I told you it was all or nothing, because it would be too complicated to be halfway. You said you were in and the next day you're kissing your ex? Why was he even here?"

She sighed, and blinked away tears. "He called and asked me to meet him. I told him that I didn't think it was a good idea, but told him he could come here. He just wanted to explain…"

"I don't care. You should have told me before he came and there was no excuse for that kiss!"

"Ash, please…"

I shook my head, got into my SUV and drove away. I left Savannah standing in front of the house with tears trailing down her face. I watched her form shrink in the rear view mirror. I didn't like seeing her sad, but I hadn't left to punish her. I left, because I knew I was losing my temper and I didn't want another accident to happen. I also wanted some time to clear my head and to make certain my reaction was warranted. I knew that it made sense for Savannah to want to hear Liam's explanation. She made a smart choice in having him come to the house, instead of meeting him somewhere. However, their kiss was burning an angry hole through my rationality.

13 REVELATIONS

Savannah

I waited outside for Ash to come back, but he didn't. Maye called me in an hour later. I retreated to my room shut the world out. My solitude would bar further complications. I worried about Ash. It was understandable for him to be angry about my kiss with Liam, but I hadn't expected the kiss. Would I ever figure out how to handle men? I couldn't help but think that the movies, pronouncing women as the confusing gender, had never been a teenage girl caught between two witches and a psychotic demon.

Later that night, I heard Ash in the hallway outside my door. His footsteps paused. I held my breath waiting for him to knock, but he continued to his room.

I picked up my mothers' journal, because I promised Willow I would study it some more and I hoped it would distract me. I hadn't picked the journal up since Izzy's mother died. My past was something I tried to keep separate from my present. I didn't want the ghostly child I once was, to haunt me. My greatest fear was myself; my past. It terrified me that my memories had the power to destroy my soul. Reading about my mother would awaken those memories.

I piled into my bed with more pillows than usual and used the light beside the bed to examine the journal. I skimmed through the parts that had nothing to do with the demon. I didn't enjoy thinking about my mother as a regular person. Reading her thoughts and worries made her seem a mere mortal. In my mind, she was an immortal executioner who continuously raked her axe against my brain stem. I couldn't escape her and I couldn't run. I was eternally bound in chains and some part of me would always be in that cage, where I watched her terminate countless lives.

My parents had decided to trap Asmodeus to gain his power. However, they first needed to learn his true name. The names of demons and angels contained power of the named one. After many failed attempts to learn Asmodeus's true name, my parents summoned the archangel, Haniel. Strangely, he was known for keeping lost secrets. He willingly gave my parents the information they needed.

I was completely immersed in my mothers' journal, when I read how they summoned Asmodeus. It was hard to believe that they hadn't ended up dead. Apparently, the name Haniel gave them was false, which amused Asmodeus. Left with no life lines, my parents had a single choice open to them; a bargain.

At first, Asmodeus wasn't interested in a bargain. After all, he was the highest ranking prince of hell; only Lucifer sat above him. However, when I crawled from my crib and into the circle, his tune changed. My mother begged him to leave me be, but Asmodeus bent down, picked me up and smelled me.

I was in shock. Asmodeus had held me as a toddler and he didn't kill me? My mother begged for my safety? This journal was going to give me a headache, while it turned my world upside down.

Asmodeus knew I was descended from the Cross lineage, but he smelled something more in my blood. He accused my mother of consorting with an angel, but she denied the accusation. Angered, Asmodeus hooked his hand around my neck and squeezed. My mother begged him to stop, but he wouldn't. My father stepped in. He shouted that I was a Nephilim and my mother looked at him in shock.

The angels had been forbidden to mate with humans, but one angel had found a loophole. To possess a human and have that human, mate with another. It wasn't technically against the rules. An angel had possessed my mother without her knowledge. My mother didn't have time to be angry with my father and rationalized that I was still her daughter. I was unique because I had three biological parents. Huh, hadn't I lucked out? Three parents and none of them stepped up to the plate to be a real parent!

The rest of the journal, was even more shocking than the realization that I had an angel for a parent. Since school had been called off, I dialed Willow and Izzy the next morning at seven. When they arrived, we secluded ourselves in my bedroom and I told them everything. They stared at me in horror, when I told them about my absentee parent, and couldn't believe that there was more.

"Asmodeus told my parents it made me stronger than the Nephilim. I was descended from the Nephilim, who had fed on the blood of a demon *and* I was also the child of an angel. He explained that it made me an entirely new species. It meant that I was more angel than human, but with demonic powers thrown into the mix."

"Geez! Girl, you have the most screwed up life ever!" Izzy said, before I finished explaining.

"Ummm… yeah!" Willow joined in the distress over my horrible life.

I sighed and continued, "Having the Cross blood was a bigger plus because it meant I was descended from the founders of two covens: Sacred Moon and Meadow Falls. Meaning I could be initiated into both, which included a massive amount of power. Asmodeus made a deal with my father. He would wait until I was old enough to be initiated into a coven. Once I was, he would use me to tap into the collective and sacrifice *every member of those covens*, me included."

"Holy Hell!" "Crap!" Izzy and Willow shouted at once.

"Yep, the story of my screwed up life continues. Apparently, my Mother didn't agree with the deal. They decided to build up enough power of their own to stop Asmodeus from taking me, but accepted that the covens would still be sacrificed. Their way of protecting me, was to sacrifice innocents to gain enough power and keep me safe." I paused, while they absorbed everything.

"Unable to internalize the power, it would be the equivalent of a nuclear bomb if they absorbed that it. *I*, on the other hand, was not a witch. As a child, they had turned their power on me. It had felt like darkness was burying into my soul, they were giving me more power. Enough power to provide protection once I could access it."

I cried. Izzy held my hand in comfort, while Willow sat behind me on the bed to wrap her arms around me in a hug. I was lucky to have two amazing friends.

"Do you think you can tell us the rest?" Willow whispered in my ear, squeezing tighter.

"Yeah, I think so."

"There's more?" Izzy was horrified, but nodded for me to continue.

"My mother wrote that their deeds to gain me power corrupted them. Their souls darkened until they remembered their goal, but not the reason behind it. They couldn't experience love any longer. Before their souls were completely lost to darkness, they threw themselves into one last act of love. They trapped the demon in the bloodstone box, hoping I would only have to call my extra power, as a last re-resort." Sobs racked my body, but Izzy and Willow helped me to gain composure.

"Shhh… it's okay. None of this is your fault."

"Yeah, Willow is right. If your parents hadn't summoned Asmodeus in the first place, none of this would have happened!"

"That's not why I am crying." Izzy handed me a Kleenex to blow my nose with. "I'm crying because this means that they loved me. They did all those horrible things because they cared. All this time, I thought they were evil, but they became that way to protect me."

The way I saw my parents was different now. They were parents who made a mistake. They were corrupted because they did the wrong thing for the right reasons. I wasn't unloved; I was loved *too much*.

"Why did the bloodstone box keep him trapped?" Willow's question made me smile. I knew she would understand my need for distraction. I leaned into her hug to show I was grateful.

"Bloodstone is a unique stone. It gives the user power over demons, while protecting them, and it destroys evil. They trapped him inside the small box. To keep the bloodstone from touching him, he had to revert to an insubstantial form. The bloodstone also made the symbols more effective. It would have perfect if I hadn't knocked the darn lid off."

The next day, Ash was still avoiding me. After the things I had learned, I wasn't up to hunting him down. Instead, I sought out the comfort of my forest. The trees were welcome friends that didn't demand anything from me. They gave me sanctuary without hesitation. I had been pushed towards a mind altering quicksand. It trickled down my throat to envelope my heart in its grainy grip. The images from my childhood were suffocating me and I needed relief.

Kit emerged, as an apparition that was far more real than the forest around me. As part of my soul, I could sense his worry for me. He rubbed his head against my skin and wrapped his tail around my legs. It was strange that he appeared as a ghost, but people could physically interact with him. I always expected my hand to pass through him, but it would come into contact with a physical body, complete with soft fur. Kits eyes glowed bright blue, his fur had a filmy black texture, but his form was mostly a silvery blue shade. He was magnificent.

I sat down with my back against a towering tree, the nearby foliage leaned over to provide a canopy of warmth. Kit arranged himself into a crescent shape with his head in my lap. His touch brought with it an intense comfort. Gone was the quicksand; Kit had chased it away. His gentle purr quieted my thoughts and I fell asleep. I must have slept for hours, because when I opened my eyes the sky was dark.

The frigid air warred with my breathe to create a milky steam, while the hairs on the back of my arms stiffened. As I started my walk back home, a branch snapped behind me. The noise originated in a shadowed area of the forest, where the trees were tightly packed together, concealing the presence of someone else. I took a step closer and saw the shadows rise from the darkness. Trembling, I took a step back and crashed into something *hard*.

Arms spun me around, slammed me into a tree, which knocked the breath from me. Asmodeus rose out of the night and came forward to press me further into the wood. His hand lay in the center of my ribcage and I worried he might shatter them with his strength.

Asmodeus leaned forth and sniffed my flesh before locking his eyes with my own. "Did you enjoy your mothers' journal?" His accent was as dark and terrifying as the rest of him. He eased the pressure on my chest and I could breathe again.

"What?"

He laughed and grinned, sardonically. "You honestly believed I wouldn't know about your little scavenger hunt? That I wouldn't watch every move you and your friends take? Oh, little *Anakim*. You have much to learn."

I recognized the term, Anakim. It was another term for the Nephilim and it bothered that he referred to me that way. "If you have been watching, then why haven't you done anything about us?"

"You think I am worried about a witchling, a human, and you? I am far more powerful than any of you." His face descended until it was less than an inch away and he snarled.

"That's not it, is it? You are weak!" I spat in his face and he used the back of his left hand to wipe it off.

"Feisty, aren't you? I am never weak. I merely don't do anything without good reason. You will learn that soon enough." I laughed. "Your insults will gain you nothing, but will cost you something." He let me go and backed away. The inscriptions along his skin shimmered and burst into a blinding glow.

"Run, little *Anakim*. I want to play." His wings spread wide. Smoke billowed off his skin and his eyes glazed over to display the fire within. I screamed and threw my strength into running. Fighting the forest, I had to carve new paths to push my way through the forest and away from him.

I found myself tangled in some branches. They tore at my skin, clothes, and hair. Refusing to give up, I push harder, but was lifted off my feet into the air. Asmodeus had me in his grip again, but this time his arms *did* crush me. Blood spilled from my lips, while the sound of my bones shattering, left an ache deep inside. Tears shed to pool on the floor beneath me. I was slipping, my mind was floating in a mist that made it difficult to concentrate, but I didn't give up. I push and kicked, though it was futile. I wasn't strong enough.

"Savannah! Wake up dammit!" A harsh smack against my cheek tore me from the nightmare. My eyes opened to find Ash standing before me. I was still leaning against the trunk and a few feet away, Kit sat next to Ash. Through our bond, I could feel Kit's confusion. I made a small attempt to send waves of comfort, but we both knew that it wasn't much of an effort.

I couldn't stop the river from flooding my eyes and spilling over onto my already moist cheeks. Kit rubbed his head against my arm, while Ash pulled me into his arms. "Kit showed up at the house without you. I followed him here. Are you okay? I thought you were injured or something!"

"Just, just hold me, please." I griped his shirt to pull him closer. Kit spirited back into my form, while Ash lifted me into his arms and carried me back to the house. I closed my eyes until I felt my bed beneath me. "Thank you."

Ash sat next to me on the bed and stared at the ground. "Don't be. You can't help your nightmares." He gave me a tiny hint of a smile and started to leave, but I grabbed his arm and pulled him back to the bed.

"That's not what I meant. I'm sorry that I kissed Liam. No matter how I rationalized it, I should not have done it. Once I knew I hurt you, I shouldn't have made excuses, because if it hurt you then it was wrong."

He looked at me when I had finished. His eyes were soft, as he leaned down to kiss me. "It's fine. I reacted too harshly. I love you, S. Now, get some rest. We can talk about this when you feel better. Okay?"

"I love you too. You know that, don't you?"

"Yeah, I think so." He folded the blanket over my body and I curled into it. I fell into a peaceful sleep after Ash left.

I woke to my phone buzzing on the nightstand. It was only six at night, but it felt much later. It was Izzy calling, but I couldn't bring myself to pick up. I hit the ignore button and fell back to sleep. I had earned a break, hadn't I?

The next morning, I climbed out of the shower and brushed the fog away from the mirror. I let out a shriek at the sight of the angry red blistering on my chest. It was in the shape of a hand; a very large hand. Panicking, I threw on some clothes and ran over to Willows house. I couldn't be alone right now. The demon had visited me in my dream and left a souvenir; a painful souvenir. He could reach through the veil of dreams to hurt me. Was there anywhere I could be safe?

Willow wasn't home, Ash was at Griffin's and I didn't want to worry Maye. I briefly thought of Izzy, but didn't want to bring up sleep and demons after the way her mother died. It would open up memories and I did not want to responsible for deepening wounds that hadn't had time to heal.

I resigned myself to decorating my room with symbols of protection. It was unlikely that they would stop Asmodeus, but they might slow him down long enough for me to get help.

When I got home, Izzy was waiting for me on my bed with her arms crossed and a caustic look on her face. "Why didn't you answer my call?"

I didn't have time to deal with drama right now. Ignoring her call one time should not earn me a trip to the land of angry Izzy. A small headache had begun to chip away at my patience. It was irritating that I would have to explain myself right now.

"I was sleeping." I pinch the area between my eyes, threw my purse to the ground, and grabbed some Tylenol from my nightstand.

"Really? Your excuse is sleep? What if my call had been urgent? What if I was in danger or I was going to commit suicide? What then?"

"Obviously that wasn't the case or we wouldn't be talking right now. Honestly, Izzy. I was half asleep and wasn't really thinking about all the bad crap you *might* calling me over. I have enough to deal with! I don't think should be angry with me over one missed call." I knew I was whining, but I felt like I was going to have a mental break down. Besides, with the stress I had been dealing with, I needed the sleep.

"Complications? That's what I am to you?" Izzy shot off the bed in anger, walked to my bookcase, took a book and threw it at me. I ducked, but another soon followed and hit me square in the chest, where the demon had burned me.

"Ow! What are you, two? You are behaving like a lunatic toddler with tantrum issues! Calm down." I closed my eyes and calmed my breathing, while Izzy did the same.

"I am not behaving like a toddler and I have good reason for acting like a nut job." Izzy's voiced sounded calm.

"Whatever your reason is, it can't compare with this." I pulled the top of my shirt down to expose my chest. Izzy gasped at the hand print. "That's why I needed rest. Okay? The demon did this and I was exhausted. I'm sorry, but I can't be expected to drop everything just because you call. You're my best friend, but I needed to take care of myself."

Izzy opened her mouth to speak, but Ash came into the room and stopped dead in his tracks. "What the…?" He looked at Izzy in shock.

"What is it? Ash? Hello, earth to planet Ash?" I waved my hand in his face, but he remained frozen.

Izzy cleared her throat. "I can tell you what's wrong with him." She smiled. I crossed my arms, waiting to hear how she had suddenly tapped into the psychic network. "He saw ghost."

"A ghost?" I laughed, hysterically. A small snort escaped to punctuate exactly what I thought of Izzy's statement "That is your explanation?"

"Um, yeah. I'm the ghost, moron." My laughter came up short and I looked more closely. Izzy form transformed into a mirage of transparency, as she stepped into a patch of sunlight. "Cool, huh? I can look real *or* I can look like a ghost." She giggled.

I knew she was serious because of her drastic mood change. She didn't look quite like Kit, but she was still a ghost. Kit materialized to examine Izzy. Izzy's unnatural acceptance of Kit caused confusion on my part. Through my body with Kit, I was able to piece together enough to know that he was able to communicate with Izzy. Evidently, communication barriers didn't exist in the spirit realm.

"How?" My voice was soft and came to a dead end with my confusion.

Ash walked over to sit on the bed with his head in his hands. Izzy stopped petting Kit and became serious. "It was the demon. That's why I called you. He came after me. I called, while running away from him. I needed your help." She shrugged.

"Oh my God!" Izzy's flippant acceptance surprised me because it was the polar opposite to my own.

"He said, he warned you that your insult would cost you something, and I was the price." Izzy took in my tears and willed her body to solidify. "Savannah, it's okay. It didn't hurt. It was quick. One moment I was alive and in a blink, I was a ghost." She gave me a hug and I clung to her.

"What is this about a Demon?" Ash spoke from the bed.
I had forgotten that Ash was in the room with us and realized that he didn't know anything about the demon. Izzy and I took turns filling him in on all the details, until Willow showed up and took over. Apparently, Izzy visited Willow before me because she wasn't remotely surprised to find two spirits in my bedroom.

14 TRACKING PREY

Ash

We attended Izzy's funeral three days after Izzy's transition into a ghost. She smoothed her form into a translucent replica, but allowed Savannah, Willow, and me to see her. We didn't tell Maye about Izzy's ghost, but I had a feeling Josephine knew. She gazed at the spot Izzy stood in, as if looking past the material world, and into the spirit realm.

Izzy's Dad, asked Savannah and Willow to sit with the family and to speak at the service. I sat with them for moral support, but I felt like a stranger. It was my first time in a church and Izzy wasn't completely dead to me. Hearing everyone cry over their loss made me feel like an insensitive spectator, because I wasn't joining them in their moist ridden grief. Izzy was as real to me as she had been a week ago.

"This is awesome! Oh my God, did you see? Triton is actually crying! Who knew he was even aware of my existence?" Izzy's laughter echoed off the painted glass, but only the three of us were aware of her. She was excited to see who really cared about her and who was attracted to the drama her funeral presented. "Get it, invisible? I'm a ghost…"

"Shhh… Stop it. This isn't funny." Willow whispered from the corner of her mouth, while Savannah glanced to see if anyone heard.

"What? I'm dead. If I have to die, I might as well enjoy it. Besides, most of these people didn't even care about me. They are only here for the pity party."

Izzy walked to her casket to see her body and let out a owlish shriek. "Ugh! Why would they put me in a pink floral dress? Shouldn't the last dress my body will ever wear, reflect me?" She looked at us in disgust, shook it off, and danced back to our bench.

The priest ran through the traditional funeral speech, while Izzy serenaded us with own version. Hers consisted of finding poking and mocking everything the priest said. It was quickly obvious that she wasn't a fan. The whole time her family had belonged to this church the priest had made her feel like the spawn of the devil. She thought it was because she dressed like a Goth, and she wasn't a fan of judgmental people.

The priest didn't miss a beat, as he talked out of his ass. "Izzy was a kind and generous girl, who touched the heart and soul of everyone she knew. She will be missed."

Playing a game of mockery with the unknowing priest, Izzy spoke in a exasperated tone. "More like, Izzy was a nice girl that everyone avoided. She had a few people who cared, but the majority will forget her once this drama has passed. Her wardrobe will be missed, but will comfort many trash bins and Goodwill." She made a disgusted sound about her wardrobe. "I can't believe my Dad threw out all of most of my clothes and gave the rest to Goodwill! I spent years putting together the perfect wardrobe. Now, it might as well rot, because it certainly won't be appreciated." She pouted and went silent.

After the service, close family and friends were invited to brunch. Willow and Savannah sat across the table from me, fidgeting with the bread on their plates, while Izzy eavesdropped on nearby conversations.

"I wish this would be over already." Savannah sounded miserable, but I was less worried about her, than I was about

Willow. Willow's sallow skin and dark puffy circles around her eyes made her look like the living dead. It was not a good sign, but I knew it was common when someone died. Even if that loved one turned into an annoying ghost, who developed a knack for stalking.

The next day, Savannah showed up at Griffins and demanded to see me. Griffin barred her from entering, but Savannah wasn't having it. She threw the force of her power against him and watched as he flew backwards into a wall.

"What the hell!" Griffin tried to stand but dizziness caused him to fall back to the floor. His ear was bleeding, but he didn't seem to notice, as he glared at Savannah in hatred.

"S, what the heck are you doing?" I pulled her away from Griffin.

"Willow is missing. She never made it home after the funeral and I'm worried. Izzy can't even find her."

"S, she probably just needed some time to herself. I'm sure she's fine." Savannah's eyes darted to Griffin before dropping her head into her hands. She was shaking in panic.

"She's probably hiding from you. Do you normally barge into people's houses and throw them into the wall? Is this a psychotic tendency I should look forward to in the future?" Griffin stood and glared at Savannah. He shot an accusing stare at me.

Savannah looked up from her hands and shouted. "Shut up!" Griffin went silent and stared in awe. Savannah turned back to face me and spoke rapidly. "No, see the coven gathered and with the murders and people going crazy…Then Josephine said she saw the sigil of death and there was blood. Oh God, there was blood!" She covered her mouth and fell against me. "I can't lose anyone else. I can't take it."

Griffin wobbled forward to put his hand on Savannahs back. It was the first time he showed her compassion. He cleared his throat. "Where was the blood?"

"Um, they found it on the porch. There wasn't a lot, but enough that we know she had an injury. The bench was turned over like something knocked into it."

Griffin nodded and looked me in the eye. "That means there was probably some kind of fight. That's good though. There's no body, which means she ran for it. The only place for her to run without anyone finding her is the forest."

"You think she's hiding in the forest?" Savannah's voice held a ray of hope. I took up Griffin's cue.

"Yeah, she probably got lost running away. We should organize a search party and comb the forest."

Savannah's posture changed from distraught to optimistic. She straightened, wiped the tears from her cheeks and kissed me. She then threw her arms around Griffin's neck and squeezed. He patted her back awkwardly and grimaced at the pain from his head injury. Griffin may be a jerk around Savannah, but he was really a good guy. Only someone who is noble would forgive someone this quickly after being blasted into the wall.

The community gathered at the coven's circle, while the local police shouted instructions on how to perform a search party. We would begin at Willow's house and spread out in a circle, while shouting her name. They told us to go in pairs and remain in sight of at least one other group, at all times.

I grabbed Savannah's shoulders, forcing her to look at me. "You told me you could take Kit's shape. Do you think you can do that now?"

Her eyes darted back and forth, but she nodded. "Why?"

"Animals are predators; they track their prey. If you change into Kit, you can smell something of Willow's and track her scent."

"You want me to go get something of hers?" Griffin's spoke gently.

Savannah nodded. "Yeah. Uh, grab the teddy bear on her bed. She sleeps with it every night and won't wash it, because it's old. She doesn't want it to lose its stitching."

Griffin raced over to Willow's house, darting between people who were pairing up for the search. I silently held Savannah until Griffin brought the teddy bear back.

"Got it. Now, where do we do this shifter thing without creeping out the regular people?"

I led them towards the shed behind Maye's house. It was for Maye's gardening tools and the size of a small bedroom. Once the door was closed, I turned to Savannah.

"Okay, now we have privacy. Work your magic."

Minutes ticked by during which, the most interesting thing that happened was a fly landing on my hand. "Come on, S. Hurry up."

"I'm trying! This is the first time. They didn't exactly give me an instruction manual."

My arms lifted in defeat and gestured for Griffin to take over. "I don't know much about shifting, but I would imagine you have to concentrate on your bond." Savannah looked at him in wonder. He shrugged. "Ash filled me in on your ability." She threw a contemptuous look my way, but focused again on Griffin. "Concentrate on your bond and immerse yourself in Kit's memories. Use his experiences to guide you through his senses. Basically, think like a panther. They're strong, fast, and great hunters. They are black and easily blend in with the night. Use all of that. Theoretically, if you immerse yourself, your body should follow the path that your mind creates."

I briefly wondered where Griffin had learned about shifting. It wasn't something that the coven taught us.

"Okay, I'll try. Just turn around and don't watch me." Neither of us turned. "I'm going to undress! I would imagine that this will rip my clothes and you boys are going to carry them, so I can change back into them when we find Willow. Turn around!"

We may have turned, but I still got a side show. There was a mirror propped against the wall of the shed, which allowed a perfect view. I wasn't trying my skills at being a peeping tom, I just wanted to watch her shift. My curiosity got the best of me, but I was still a man, who liked what he saw.

For a long while, nothing happened and then came the seizure. Black threads multiplied and spread across her skin in a maze. The threads transformed into fur, as they burst through her flesh. Her eyes widened and grew. The bones in her back broke and set in new ways. Her face resembled a kaleidoscope, as it shifted into its new setting. The whole process looked painful, but in way it was also beautiful.

With each crack of her bones, I could feel Griffin cringe beside me. Savannah didn't make sounds of distress, but when the process was finished she growled. I turned around to take in Savannah in her feline form. As a ghost, Kit had blue eyes, but Savannah as a panther had bright yellow eyes. She was 8 feet long with sleek black fur.

Her roar rattled the shed. She shook her head and approached Griffin to sniff the bear in his hand. Nervous, he backed away. "Man, this is weird. Savannah, you know all those times I was an ass, I was just kidding." He laughed and looked me in the eye. "She could tear my throat out." He loosened the neckline of his shirt and opened the shed door. Everyone else had already entered the forest.

"S, if you can understand me lick my right hand." I held my hands near her, fighting my instincts to run from her predatory form. She flicked out her tongue, catching the barest hint of my skin. "Okay, you track her and we will follow. Just, make sure we're able to keep up, okay?" She snorted and raced off with us following.

I couldn't believe how fast she was. She tore through the forest, easily maneuvering around each obstacle. Unfortunately, she had to pause repeatedly for us to catch up. Often we would watch from a distance, while she climbed trees to lie on a branch.

Griffin and I were exhausted from running through the woods, when Savannah halted. She started circling, which reminded me of a cat chasing its tail. However, the anxiety coming off her in waves was vastly different than the playful attitude of a kitten.

"What's wrong with her?" Griffin crouched near Savannah, while I searched the surrounding woods. "Ah. Here's her problem." I looked back to see Savannah nosing aside some leaves. Griffin lifted a leaf for me to see; droplets of blood smeared the waxy surface.

"Damn." Savannah's eyes glowed at me before she turned and sprinted away. We followed until she slowed. Her form began to slink low to the ground like a cat does when stalking prey. A head of us, I could make out the shape of a shed and realized it was the shed Willow and Savannah used to play in as children. My stomach clenched. What if Willow was dead too?

We neared the shed and Savannah sniffed around the edges. I opened the door, but it was empty.

"S, she's not here."

She let loose a deafening roar and starting using her paws to dig at the dirt around the shed. I looked closer and saw that there was a large cavern underneath, which the shed had been built on. Savannah was attempting to pull the dirt enough to squeeze through the opening. She wiggled her head through until only her body remained on the outside. That was when we heard the scream. It was loud enough that I thought an animal must be dying, but I could recognize the tone as Willow's.

Savannah's efforts increased, while I bent down to help push her through. Griffin and I soon followed. The cavern was a tiny basement to the shed, but large enough for the four of us to fit in. Griffin took out his cell phone to light up the surrounding area.

Willow was against the far wall; trying to shrink into it. Her skin was covered in layers of dirt, while clumps of mud and stray branches peppered her hair. Her nails were red from clawing at the wall behind her. She had left some decent sized abrasions in the wall.

Willow didn't seem to recognize us. Her head shook back and forth, while her hands tore at her hair and cry's racked her body. Griffin and I inched away from her, while Savannah moved forward. Willows picked up a rock and threw it at Savannah hitting her in the head.

Savannah whimpered, lowered herself to the ground and slowly inched forward. Her paws were outstretched and Willow watched like a hawk. Rolling onto her back, Savannah began to rock from side to side. She was trying to convey her harmless nature and Willow seemed entranced enough to allow Savannah near. For her last roll, Savannah ended up next to Willow and lifted her head. She moved forward and licked a large gash on Willows arm.

The sound that burst from Willow was one of defeat and acceptance. She pulled Savannah onto her lap and held her. Slowly, Savannah's body changed until she was naked in Willow's arms. She then moved to hold Willow and gently rocked her until she quieted.

"Shhh... Willow, everything's fine. No one is going to hurt you. I'll keep you safe, I promise."

"Me too." Their heads snapped up at Izzy's voice and Willow's eyes held recognition.

Willow looked at each of us in turn and took in Savannah's naked state. "Why are you naked?" We all laughed.

"When I shift, I don't get to take my clothes with me. I didn't think it was a good idea to take the time for clothes, when you obviously needed me."

"Oh."

I handed Savannah her clothes, which she quickly put on. Willow allowed me to help her up and out from under the shed. On the way back to the search party, she explained that the demon had been in her head. If was telling her to kill someone and without knowing what else to do, she slammed her head into the porch. Her rationality had fled; she just wanted him out of her head.

Once she injured herself, the demons voice stopped. However, when she turned, she found him standing across the street and ran for the forest. She hid beneath the shed because she knew Savannah would find her.

Savannah

I wanted to tear him limb from limb. I was so furious that I had half a mind to hunt down the demon. However, Willow's mind was weakened by his onslaught and I couldn't stand to leave her so soon. We each took a shower and curled on her day bed. She was shivering and kept moving her hand to make sure I was still next to her.

Why did Asmodeus want to take everything from me? Hadn't he had enough? I ached inside at how terrified Willow had been, and the thought that she suffered through it alone, while I searched for her. Izzy stayed with us, but sat near the window watching the moon. Kit sat next to her. These were my two best friends; my family. I couldn't allow him destroy my world.

I had spent my childhood being led on a leash through each trial. When I came to live with Maye, I promised myself that I wouldn't allow my world to be dictated. This was five steps further than dictating my life; he had turned me into a puppet, while he created the stage.

"I can't let him do this anymore." I was hardly aware I spoke aloud, but Izzy turned to face me and Willow sat up. "He's going to keep going until he kills everyone. That's what the journal said. My parent's killed all of those people to give me enough power to stand up to him. I think it's about time I did."

"Are you crazy? All he has to do is wiggle into your brain and pop goes the weasel."

"Izzy, I don't think that helps anything." Willow's voice shook. "Savannah, I know you feel responsible, but going all superhero on his ass isn't going to help matters. He's too strong."

"Did you really just say *ass*?" Izzy laughed until it turned into a mad giggle. Willow responded by grabbing her teddy and throwing it at Izzy, but it merely passed through her to hit the window. "Ha! You can't hit me unless I let you." They demonstrated their maturity by sticking their tongues out at one another.

"Seriously, you guys! What else am I supposed to do? I can't sit around while he kills people. Willow could have died and Izzy, you already have." The three of us were silent, while we each thought about everything that had happened. "This isn't a discussion, okay? I *am* taking this fight to him. There is no doubt about that. I just need to figure out how to do it. You can help me make a plan or stand by and watch. Either way, I have made my decision."

15 INTERVENTION

Ash

I slept until noon the next day and found Savannah's bed empty. Maye was at an elder gathering and knowing Savannah, she was at Willow's. I walked over to Willows intending to offer some solace, but when I got there I was marooned in the living room.

"Hi." I turned to find Willow standing alone.

"Um, is Savannah here?"

"She's still sleeping." I gave her a confused glance, since Savannah never slept past noon before. "I placed some herbs in her breakfast to make her sleep. She didn't get any last night."

"Oh. I tell her I was here." I began to leave, but Willow stopped me.

"She's going to get herself killed. She wants to go after him, alone." I halted, but didn't turn to face her. "She thinks she can do it by herself, but she can't. She will only allow me and Izzy to help her create a plan, but wants us to remain behind when she goes after him."

"I won't let her." I tuned my head slightly, while I spoke and walked out the door.

"I know. That's why I told you." She closed and locked the door behind me.

My mind went through all of the possible scenarios and realized that Savannah is too stubborn for me to stop her. However, I could help her. Obviously, she didn't want the coven in on this. I could understand that. With that many people, it would turn into a massacre. Besides, most of the coven was against using their power in such a way. That left me two choices; Griffin or Liam.

I got in my car and drove. I knew where to go, because Maye insisted on knowing Liam's address when Savannah dated him. I memorized it the first time she gave it to me. He opened on my first knock and I gave him credit for not wearing a surprised expression. He merely opened the door and stepped aside for me to enter.

"I'm sure there is a good reason for you being here? Decide you need to attack me again? Maybe you want to piss outside my door to mark your territory?"

"Savannah is in trouble." Liam's attitude went from sarcastic to serious in the space of seconds. I sighed. "Look, we hate each other. It doesn't take a genius to figure that much out, but we care about Savannah. If I am going to keep her safe, I am going to need more than a witchling, ghost, and spirit animal."

"What do you need?"

Liam

If Ash showing up at my place wasn't bad enough, the news he came with was much worse. My head pounded from everything he told me. We managed to agree that we would confront Savannah about her plan and the stupidity behind it. Willow and Izzy were already on board. After we developed our intervention, we went to railroad Savannah into being part of a plan, rather than the sole participant.

We found Savannah rifling through boxes in the attic. It was a tight fit, but we all managed to squeeze into it.

"What now?" Savannah's lips took on an angry pout that was completely kissable.

I expected Ash to take the lead, but Willow stepped up to the plate before him. "We are here to help and not just with the plan, but the execution of it." Willow gave Savannah a sarcastic smile, and said "This is not a discussion. *We* are confronting him and we are creating the plan. You can help or stand back, while we take care of everything. Sound familiar?"

Savannah smiled. "Do you have to use my own words against me? I suppose this means that the boys have been filled in on everything?"

"Yeah." Willow glanced at everyone in confusion. "You're not going to argue? You know, tell us we can't help or something? I had an argument all planned out!"

"You're angry that you don't get to argue? Typical!" Izzy shouted from behind all of us.

"Willow, I know you better than you realize. I knew you were going to stand by; I just hoped you would. You're going to do this against my will, but if I work with you... I might be able to keep you all safe. God, you make me seem so irrational sometimes."

Savannah shook her head and went back to digging around in random boxes. We all chipped in and brought the items we found to Savannah's room. The girls placed the items on the bed and waited for Savannah to talk.

"Alright, I am building my plan based on my mothers' journal. Bloodstone is the key here. Obviously, it works since it trapped him. Now, my theory is that if we managed to get the bloodstone inside him, we might be able to kill him. I mean, my mother said he couldn't even touch the stuff." She shrugged, sat on her bed, and leaned on her pillows.

"That's it." I couldn't help it, but her plan seemed a little bland. "How are you doing to get it inside him? How are you going to live long enough to get that close? Oh, and what if it doesn't work?"

Ash spoke from beside me. "Easy, the plan doesn't work; we die. Then the covens both die and its celebration time in hell."

He walked over to a box with bloodstone decorated across it. "What if we made a bloodstone dagger? If we did that, it could puncture his skin."

"Liam's right, though. How do we get close enough? He's strong." Willow fidgeted with the sleeves of her shirt and I could see she was frightened.

"My panther; I'm strong in that form and fast. I can take care of him physically, while you guys attack him magically. One of us just needs to get close enough to stab him, while he is distracted by the others."

"Still a problem guys" Izzy spoke from the corner. "How exactly do we make a bloodstone dagger?" We looked at one another and not a single one of us put forth an idea.

"You make it with light and dark magic and forge it in the essence of a spirit." Unanimously, we turned in horror to find Maye standing in the doorway. "You honestly believe I have remained oblivious to everything that's going on? Give me some credit."

"Maye, you know? How?" Ash moved closer to Savannah and sat beside her on the bed. Savannah placed her hand over his mouth and spoke. "We have to do this. Please, don't try to stop us." She pleaded.

Maye gave us a warm smile. "I'm not going to stop you; I'm going to help you. Liam, Ash, Izzy come with me. I will need all three of you if we are going to make this dagger. Savannah, go outside and practice maneuvers as a she-panther. Willow, watch her and practice some moves of your own."

No one moved. "If you all want to stop this thing, we better get moving. I'm a lot slower than I used to be. I'm no spring chicken." She cracked a smile and went downstairs.

"She seems smart." I felt stupid saying it, but I needed to break the silence.

"Yeah." Everyone else spoke at once.

Izzy, Ash, and I trailed downstairs to find Maye. We left Willow and Savannah alone in the bedroom with shocked expressions still frozen on their faces. Maye brought us downstairs and into the basement. She signaled for us to come closer and moved aside a painting to reveal a small handle. She turned it and the wall opened up into a study.

"Come on in." Maye smiled back at us.

We filed into the room; Ash sat in a velvet chair beside an antique cabinet. Izzy took up the space behind the chair and I leaned against the wall we came through.

"Now, if I heard right, you need to make a weapon from bloodstone?" We nodded. "I have just the thing." She opened a large trunk and took out a large box, which she set on the desk. Unlatching the box, she opened it to reveal a scabbard inlaid with ivory. She pulled a straight edged dagger from the sheath. "This is a stiletto. It's Italian."

Maye handed the stiletto to me. The blade was sharp with decorative inscriptions along it. The hilt was shaped like a triton and was perfectly balanced with the blade. It wasn't an overly decorative dagger, but it looked deadly.

"What are you doing with a dagger?" Ash leaned forward with a worried expression. "I thought you didn't believe in violence?"

"Just because I don't believe in violence, doesn't mean I don't believe in protecting the ones I love. Besides, I've never used it."

"Okay, does anyone else think it's totally cool that Maye owns a dagger? I mean, talk about crazy!" Izzy spoke and then shrieked in excitement. "So, how do we do this?"

Ash and I used our magic to encase the blade in a thin layer of bloodstone from a large chunk that Maye provided us with. We left the sharp edges untouched to allow for easy puncture. We then followed several rituals to destroy and ward off evil. When we were finished, Maye looked to Izzy.

"What? What am I supposed to do?" Izzy waved her hands in the air. "I'm a ghost remember? I'm pretty useless."

Maye shook her head in amusement and walked with the dagger to Izzy. She then waved the dagger through Izzy's insubstantial form and held it where Izzy's heart would have been. Izzy gasped in amazement.

"That tickles!" She bent over laughing and Maye removed the stiletto. It no longer gave the impression of bloodstone. The center of the blade held a deep metallic blue shimmer, while the edges glowed white.

Looking at the dagger in awe, Maye spoke quietly against the blade. "Kissed by Death." Maye's words brought the blade to life. When she moved, the air gave it a fiery embellishment. "That is the blades name." She walked to Ash and handed it to him. He took it carefully. "Savannah must be the one to wield it. I expect you to make certain she doesn't get herself killed doing it."

"I'll protect her." He nodded seriously and slipped the blade into the scabbard.

Savannah

Willow and I sat outside, wondering what the others were doing. It was strange that Maye already knew everything, but even more bizarre was the fact that she wasn't stopping us. Why hadn't she said anything before?

"S, we have the dagger." I turned to see everyone coming outside, while Ash handed me the dagger. I looked at the blade and thought it was pretty, but it didn't look anything like bloodstone.

"Guys, I thought you were supposed to make a *bloodstone* dagger. This is… I don't know what this is."

"S, believe me, it's bloodstone. It just looks different because Izzy blessed it or something.

"Oh. Okay." I examined the dagger more closely and sat back on the grass beside Willow. The world felt like it had slowed to a snail's pace. Our plans suddenly seemed real. Thinking about them and executing them were entirely different. Everyone seemed hesitant to break the silence, but Maye stepped forward and severed the string. She effectively pushed us over the cliff into the arms of the future; we just didn't know what that future would be.

"You have the tool. Now, you just need to figure out how to bring Asmodeus to you and how to keep him there long enough to kill him."

"Maye." I shouted before she could leave. "Why are you letting us do this?" She turned back to look at our group.

"I'm not *letting* you do anything. If I told you not to, you wouldn't listen. I'm choosing to support you in the decision you have made. I'll still be waiting inside with Josephine. I will probably end up baking a kitchen worth of baked goods, while worrying over all of you. There is a definitely possibility that I will wear the carpets down with my pacing." Maye walked forward and held my cheeks.

"Darling, you and Ash are my world. Josephine warned me that this was going to happen. I had to stand by and let the pieces fall where they may. I love you." Maye hugged each of us in turn and walked back inside.

"Have any good ideas?" Liam spoke while the rest of us remained in awe at Maye's reaction.

Willow chipped in her two cents. "Well, I guess we could summon him…"

I knew that would bring Asmodeus to us, but I was worried that the coven could get hurt. "If we did it in the forest, we wouldn't have to worry about anyone getting caught in the middle."

Everyone agree, we spent the afternoon hammering out the details and the part each of us would play. We decided that the following evening would be the right time to put our plan in place. The sooner; the better.

16 TO LIVE OR DIE

Savannah

We choose our playground and set the stage. Liam, Ash, and Willow would attack Asmodeus with their magic, while I distracted him in my panther form. We needed to keep Asmodeus on the defense. Once we had him sufficiently distracted, I would shift back into my natural form and stab Asmodeus. Izzy's job was to keep hold of the dagger and hand it to me, when the time came.

It was easy to set up the circle to summon Asmodeus. Since we had done it before, the guys let us take the lead. They seemed shocked at the full force of the whirlpool. It was stronger outside than it had been in Izzy's apartment. Nature enhanced the summoning, and the winds the whirlpool created seemed had the intensity of a hurricane.

We expected the demon to show itself, but we didn't expect that he wouldn't appear within the circle. Instead, he took corporeal form behind Liam. He used one arm to send Liam flying through the air until he hit a tree trunk with a resounding crack. The other arm gestured towards the circle and pulled the energy into his palm.

Asmodeus smiled, while his hand held an enormous ball of energy. His head twitched back and forth, as it had in the secret passageway. His eyes sought mine and in the space of seconds he conveyed his amusement at our attempt to confront him. My stomach dropped when his head turned to Ash and he sent the energy ball flying towards him.

The ball hit Ash in the chest and I expected him to fly backwards, but the ball transformed into vines, which wrapped around his ribcage. They started tightening at a slow, agonizing pace. I focused on transforming into my panther form. Meanwhile, Willow called on Earth. The roots of the surrounding trees sprung up through the dirt, at Asmodeus' feet and grabbed his wrists before he could do any more harm. Asmodeus merely laughed at her attempt and broke the restraints.

Liam shook the pain from his injured body and sent an ice storm towards Asmodeus. I urged my body to shift more quickly and watched as the ice climbed through the feathers of Asmodeus' wings. In response, Asmodeus snapped his wings open and sent icicles flying in all directions. One caught Liam in his arm, but he continued his fight.

I burst forth as a panther, sinking my teeth into the Arch demon's feet and dragging until he fell backwards. Switching tactics, I went for his wings and repeatedly bit, until I was certain they were damaged enough to prevent flying. His blood tasted different than I expected. It was warm and rich when I thought it would be stale and tar-like.

"Willow!" Liam shouted. I looked towards her to see a tiger made entirely of fire. Liam created a wall of ice between Willow and the tiger, but her arms had already been badly burnt from trying to fend it off.

Asmodeus shook me off, which knocked the wind out of me. He walked towards Willow, who was now standing with Liam. Ash lay on the ground beside them; his face blue and the vines wrapped tightly around him. His mouth was frozen in a silent scream and his eyes were dead. My heart broke and I roared with all the pain this demon had brought into my life.

I stalked Asmodeus; not wanting to signal my approach and threw my whole body against his back. My teeth reached for his throat. Finding skin, I bit down with all the force I could muster. A sound tore through him that I recognized as a scream, but sounded closer to a terrifying song.

Asmodeus threw me off him and crouched. His face was twisted in anger, his eyes blazed with an inner fire, and his skin electrified with inscriptions.

"I will kill you for that!" He bared his teeth and I saw each of them was sharpened to fine points. I roared in response; begging him to try. A slow, wicked smile lit up his face; showing me that he understood my dare. My paws inched backwards, while his feet replaced the ground I gave up. I turned and ran; he pursued.

He was fast, but I had the strength of a panther behind my movements. I needed him to follow me. Ash was already dead, Willow badly wounded, and Liam's injured was more extensive than I originally thought. I wouldn't let him hurt anyone else I loved.

Izzy appeared in my path with the dagger. I shifted as quickly as possible and took the blade in my hands. She handed me my dress, which I threw on as I ran. It was dark and though I could hear his laughter behind me, I was terrified of making a wrong turn.

I was a mouse in a wooded maze. Asmodeus laughed as I made a futile attempt to escape, but only he knew the way out. He didn't count on the fact that I never intended to find my way out. I was fighting for the survival of my loved ones now. I didn't care if I lived or died, but I *needed* them to. If this would be my last stand, I could die with that. I refused to stop even though my veins melted away to acidic fire. I needed freedom from the cage he had made of my life. I needed to have a choice.

My dress strap caught on a branch and was torn free causing minor pain, when the edge pressed into my shoulder and drew blood. Chaotic laughter trailed behind me. The ageless trees loomed around me to conceal this creature, which would destroy everyone I loved. Their branches attempted to restrain my wrists, while their roots shackled my ankles. I clawed at the barriers until I came to a dead end. I had made a *wrong turn*.

Towering rocks trapped me between them and *him*. My attempt to climb them proved useless, which left me a single option. I turned to meet him in the dance of death. One of us would die tonight. I tore the dagger from the scabbard and threw the scabbard into the forest. I took a fighting stance and *waited*.

17 ULTIMATUM

Liam

Willow leaned over Ash's body and tore the vines from him. Tears carved their passage down her cheeks to bathe his face. I sat inches away holding my shirt to the wound from the icicle. I wanted to go after Savannah, but I knew I would be a liability. I tried to comfort Willow, but she pushed me away.

Willow gently lifted Ash's head and bent her head to kiss his lips. I thought she was saying her goodbyes, but her body began to spasm. Her limbs tightened and relaxed in patterns, while she pulled his lips open. The spasms moved from the lower half of her body to the top in waves.

When the waves reached her neck, a long trail of green smoke trailed from her mouth like a snake. Its head moved clockwise around his lips and dipped into his mouth, similarly to how a child tests the water with their toes before diving in. The snake plunged into Ash's mouth and down his throat.

I felt sick, as I watched the snake's tail emerge from Willow's mouth to swim into Ash's. It caused Ash's throat to expand with its size. Once the snake had left her completely, Willow collapsed beside Ash. Her chest continued to swell with each breath she took.

Ash's body jerked. His eyes opened to reveal white sockets, while his chest twitched with electricity that ran along his skin. His body curled into the fetal position and wiped back, until I thought his spine would split in half.

Willow woke and scooted away from Ash's body in horror. Her hand covered her mouth and a sound tore from her chest. It was a familiar sound; almost comforting. Though, I wasn't anxious for her call to be answered.

The ground shook with the full force of her call. The air behind Ash turned into a minor cyclone; pulling debris into its vortex. I stood, still holding my wound and limped over to Willow. She finally quieted, but it was already too late. Death stepped through the vortex and walked forward.

With each step he took, the plants at his feet blackened and decayed. He was furious. Ash's eyes blinked open. He sat up in amazement, but when he saw Death approach him, he did what any sane man would do; he moved away.

Behind Death, Kali and her sister Ivy came through the portal and it closed behind them. Ivy was smaller than her sisters. She had a petite frame, but was quick. Her Hellhound name was Poison, which suited her personality. Though, her appearance did not. She was a platinum blond with a vivacious body.

I cleared my throat. "What brings you three to my neck of the woods?"

Death flipped his head in my direction to assess me. He looked like an ordinary man; brown hair, onyx eyes, tall, and well built. However, he had such an intensity that no mortal could be in his presence without fear. This was *Death*; the one thing that all living beings avoided and feared.

"Silence." Death turned to face Willow. "What makes you think that you have the right to command death?" His voice was hollow; like the absence of sound and yet we all heard him.

"I… If I have the power to do it that gives me the right." She stood and placed herself between Ash and Death. "*You* are not going anywhere near him!"

Death stopped and appraised Willow. "A mortal thinks she can stop death?" He laughed.

"Willow let him through." It was Kali who spoke and she looked humble. I had never seen her this way before. It was as though all life had been sucked from her and she was merely a dog, lapping at Death's heels. Ivy stood beside her with a domineering smile.

"No. Got it? I don't care what you are. I gave him life and you are *not* taking it away!" Willow moved forward until her face was even with Death's shoulders. He looked down, but his anger had evaporated. He seemed amused and it was confirmed, when he doubled over, holding his stomach from laughing.

The hellhounds looked on in horror, but Death's laughter only made Willow angrier. When had she gotten a backbone?

"Don't laugh at me!" She smacked Death across the face and everyone froze, while Willow's face transformed into one of shock. "Oh my God, I... I didn't mean to. I'm sorry. I've never hit anyone before. Are you okay?"

Willow moved forward in concern and tilted his head up to inspect her handiwork. A red welt was already swelling where she hit him. She caressed his cheek and we all watched, while she healed the injury she had caused.

Death's eyes narrowed to slits. He grabbed Willow around the throat, dragged her to him, and then bit her neck. Blood trailed down her collarbone.

"Please, she didn't know any better!" Kali rushed forward begging Death. "Don't hurt her! She's just a child!"

Death lifted his head from Willow's neck and licked the blood that had pooled at her collarbone. "Why did you heal me?"

"I hurt you. I believe in fixing your own messes. Now, I think I would like to give you a new slap and *not* heal it!" Her hand reached up to repeat her earlier gesture, but he caught it and yanked her to him.

"Do you know what you are?" Death gazed in her eyes and nodded to Ash. "You have the power to give life. It's a power that resides with me...*and* those who I gift with it. There is only one Hellhound I ever gifted with that power and she is long since dead."

"Well, obviously you have your wires crossed, because I just *gave* him life." Willow pulled her wrist from his grip and crossed her arms.

"Hasn't anyone ever taught you to respect others?" Death reached out his arm to bar Kali, when she tried to go to Willow.

"I'll respect you when you earn it, but it still won't change anything. You *will* leave Ash alone."

Death sighed, and Ivy laughed in the background. "It seems we are at an impasse. The only way you could have the gift to give life, is if you are a direct descendant of the hellhound I gave the gift to. I wasn't aware any of her offspring survived." He turned to look at Kali and Ivy, who shook their heads.

"I don't care *who* I am a descendant of. I want you to leave."

Death raised his eyebrows at Willow's voice. "You think you can order death? His soul is mine. He died and I came to claim him. Although, I might be willing to make a deal."

Willow shot a nervous look in my direction, but shook it off quickly to face Death. "What kind of deal?"

"I only have five remaining hellhounds. All of the others have died and they rarely give birth. I could use another. If you agree to join my ranks and take your place among your sisters, I will allow your witch to live."

"What if I say no?"

"There are many ways to kill someone. Your witch might fall down the stairs and break his neck or a bus may hit him, while crossing the street. You can't be with him all the time." A crooked smile lit up his features and I shivered.

"I have friends and a family. Ask for something else."

"No." He snapped his fingers and a large tree branch fell next to Ash. "That could have been his head."

Tears fell from Willow's eyes, while she took in Ash and the enormous branch beside him.

"Willow, don't do it. It's okay. If I was meant to die...I can face that." Ash stood and attempted to push Willow out of the way. She turned and looked Death in the eye.

"Give me until the end of summer to give you my decision." When Death opened his mouth to speak, she placed her hand over his lips to silence him. "If he's as easy to kill as you claim, you can wait." His eyes crinkled in amusement and he nodded.

"You have a deal." A sigil appeared on Willow's inner wrist, in sync with Death's words. Ivy howled to open a portal and they left.

I was alone in a clearing with Willow and Ash, but Izzy soon appeared to remind us that Savannah was facing an Archdemon on her own. I wasn't sure how much time had passed.

"I gave her the dagger." Izzy spoke quickly. "Well, come on. We can't let her face this on her own!"

Her words pushed us into action. Izzy blinked out of sight, while the three of us raced in the direction Savannah had gone in. She went off the trail we originally set out and it slowed us down, because we had to track her.

18 CHOICES

Savannah

I stood poised for Asmodeus's attack, waiting for him to barrel through the woods and attack me head on. He walked through the trees and leaned casually against a tree. His neck, ankle, and wing had completely healed. Our efforts hadn't even put a dent in his armor. It was insulting.

"That's a pretty little blade you have there, but it won't help you."

"We'll just see about that."

Asmodeus shrugged nonchalantly. "As you wish, you can't surprise me though. I've been watching you all along. I know all of your little secrets. It's what I do. I have always believed in the need to know your enemy."

"Oh really? You think you know *all* my secrets? Why? Because you slip in my dreams and stalk my friends?"

I made my move. I lunged with my dagger, but he danced aside. His moves were smooth and graceful. It looked effortless. I had never been a fighter, but I knew the basics. I threw a punch with my free hand, but he caught my fist. Throwing my weight into my movement, I attempted to stab him in the gut and deliver a kick to the groin, but he spun around and caught me in a choke hold.

"You think I stalk your friends and haunt your dreams? You think that is the only way I've been able to watch you?" He laughed hysterically and tightened the choke hold. "How about we play a game of trivia? What is one of the first things people learn about demons?"

"I'm not going to play your stupid game!" I felt dizzy from lack of oxygen.

"Play or I will fly to your friends faster than your little panther can run. I'll kill them all and then I will continue on to take each coven."

"I don't know. What is it?" I barely managed to choke the words out. He let go and walked a few paces away to sit on a large boulder.

"Think about it."

I struggled to answer the question, racking my brain for all of the stereotypes. "Ah, crosses and holy water hurt them?" He nodded. "They work for the devil and live in hell." Again, he nodded. "A priest exorcizes them."

"Bingo. Now, why does a priest exorcize them?"

I was beginning to feel like a child and I didn't like it. I sighed, "They exorcize demons because the demon possesses someone." Asmodeus smiled. It was an eerie smile that left spiders crawling up my spine. "You... you possessed someone I know?" In shock, I thought about all of the people in my life. "Who? Isis? Griffin?" My throat tightened. "Willow?"

"Your lover boys. You see, it really wasn't that difficult. Whenever you were with them, I slipped in to take over. They didn't even realize they had become my puppets."

I felt ill. Thinking over the past few weeks and how fickle I had been, the sudden surge in hormones I had never experienced before. How I sometimes felt a magnetism pushing me towards Liam or Ash, while other times I didn't... I loved both of them. I was in love with Ash; Ash who I had never viewed as anything other than a brother... until recently.

"I used my power to lure you to me and played on your desires."

Tears fell before I could stop them. My vision swam when I looked Asmodeus in the eyes. His wings were open and his inscriptions had faded to a poor example of their true worth. I could feel it; the way I felt when I was alone with Ash or Liam. The overwhelming wave of energy that pulled me towards them, I felt it with *Asmodeus*.

"No! It can't be." I shook my head and backed away with my hands held out in front of me, as if barring the truth from touching me. "It wasn't you! I... Oh God. Why? Why did you do this? Couldn't you have just killed me?" I covered my mouth with my hand in disbelief. "If you just wanted my power, why play with me like this?"

"I needed to keep an eye on you. After all, I needed time to gain enough energy to keep my physical form. Besides, it kept me amused. Still want to kill me?"

My hand holding the dagger dropped to my side in defeat. I was in love with an Archdemon, who not only wanted to kill me, but everyone I loved. He was a murder, who ruled in hell alongside Lucifer. I thought back to each time I saw Asmodeus in person or my dreams. Then I thought about the moments I experienced with Ash and Liam, but those moments were with *him*. How could I kill someone I was in love with?

Asmodeus pushed off his rock to walk over to me. He looked me in the eyes, reached out, and pulled me to him. In his arms, I felt the pressure build. His eyes softened to a downy blue and he leaned downward to press me into a savage kiss. It was intense and I couldn't stop my body from betraying my mind. I responded to him with all the hunger I could.

Asmodeus pushed me into the rocky structure behind me and wrapped us in his wings. He tore at my dress, snapped the remaining strap, and nibbled on my earlobe.

"Oh God, I want you." His teeth broke the flesh of my neck and he fed from me. I wanted more. I wanted to taste every piece of him. I was betraying everything I stood for. He would kill us all and I was going to let him, because my silly heart wouldn't listen to my brain.

I heard my friends shouting in the distance. They were looking for me. Asmodeus lifted his head in the direction of their voices. "I'll be back." He moved to go after them, but I plunged the dagger deep into his chest. His head swung back in surprise, while blood spurted between his lips and he looked down.

I cried, even while I knew he was evil, I couldn't help but love him. "I'm sorry. I can't let you hurt anyone else."

Asmodeus stumbled backwards, pulled the dagger from his chest and let it fall to the ground. His body began to shimmer like a dying fairy. He was corporeal one moment and the next, he wasn't. He walked forward to place my hand over his wound. His eyes looked ordinary now and the inscriptions had faded from his chest. He looked like a man, a dying man. He wiped my tears away with his fingertips and when I closed my eyes, he kissed my eyelids. Uncontrollable sobs overtook me, and I started to hyperventilate.

Asmodeus placed his index finger over my lips, but it was insubstantial and passed right through me. He leaned forward, until his lips were next to my ear and whispered. "Thank you. It would have been a shame to kill you. Be safe, my little Anakim." Before he could move back enough to look me in the eyes, he disappeared.

I fell to the ground, screaming at the sky. Every cherished moment I spent loving Liam and Ash, I had really loved a monster. My entire childhood had been one huge nightmare, but it had been my parents' way of protecting me. Izzy and Ash were dead. I was a virus; I destroyed everything I touched. I brought this evil to this place and into the lives of everyone I loved. Why did everyone else die, while I lived?

The shouting in the distance had grown louder, they were getting closer. I started to panic until my eyes fell on the dagger, abandoned on the ground. It was still fresh with Asmodeus' blood. Gripping it in my hand, I angled the blade towards me. The horrors that had been visited on me throughout my life, were too much to take any longer. I couldn't continue to watch this world die a slow, painful death that I brought with me.

My tears froze and for the first time I felt in control. I could decide; this was my choice. I moved the dagger far from my body and plunged it inward. The anger, pain, betrayal was all gone. My world was clear and I was free. This was what a choice was. Fate did not command me, my parents' choices had not forsaken me, I was just *me*. This was my world, those were my friends, and the darkness couldn't touch me unless I gave it permission. I looked down at the dagger sticking out of my torn dress. What was one more hole?

Willow walked into the clearing, while everyone else trailed behind her. She saw my hand covered in blood gripping the dagger, and screamed. Running forward, she grabbed my hands to pull them away from the wound.

"It's not mine."

Her eyes search mine in confusion. "I don't understand."

"The blood is Asmodeus's. I made a choice; to live. The dagger is stuck in my dress, but only next to my skin. It's not in my skin." I smile awkwardly, while my friends looked at me in horror. "I needed to take back control. I had to *want* to live or I never would."

I stood and walked to Ash. I cupped his cheek, but didn't feel anything. My emotions were as they should be and the same was true for Liam. "I'm glad everyone is okay." My voice sounded strange. I was no longer weighted down. When I smiled at my friends, my family… it was the first true smile of my *life*.

ABOUT THE AUTHOR

J.D. Stroube is a debut author, who will be releasing several novels in the near future. She spends most of her free time with her family, writing, and reading. As an animal lover, she often visits pet shops and shelters to play with the animals. She is also teaching herself how to do photomanipulations.

Visit her website: http://jdstroube.weebly.com/

10052500R0012

Made in the USA
Charleston, SC
03 November 2011